By
J. P. Leonard

Never Die On A Cold Night II
REVELATIONS

The characters and events in this book are fictitious and not based on any real persons living or dead.

By
J. P. Leonard

My work is dedicated to the woman who has always been there for me…my wife.

Never Die On A Cold Night II
REVELATIONS

CHAPTER ONE

"A Ball of Confusion"

The scene viewed by Officer Darren Wilson crawled with police and the FBI. It was quite cold later that afternoon, but it didn't stop the usual hustle and bustle on the streets of Chicago. Traffic was tied up, and extra uniformed police had to be called in to re-route it and to keep it moving. Although the cold made it hard for people to breathe, you could still smell the scent of fire mingled with the scent of burnt flesh. The firefighters were working feverishly to control the flames engulfing both vehicles. Some brave officer was trying to move the car from between the two burning police cars. Finally, the firefighters put out the blaze. Charley and Judith made it to the scene almost simultaneously. As they walked around the scene, trying not to get in each other's way, they looked at the remains of the police officers who had been the arresting team. The captain was sitting on the back bumper of one of the ambulances getting his head bandaged and ointment placed on a nasty cut on his arm. Officer Darren Wilson walked over to Charley, "I talked to the witnesses on the scene, and they all say the same thing. A black van with two shooters armed with grenade launchers fired on the two police cars, but they never fired on the car Detective Neal occupied. They just passed it by," Officer Wilson explained.

"What about the cops who were in the car with David? Where are they?"

"I don't know, Charley. Maybe they chased David after he got away." Officer Wilson said, giving his speculation as to what had happened. "Look at the rear-side window where they must have had him. The window is busted out. Maybe they went after him and got whacked."

"Well, you better put an APB out on the cops and Detective Neal."

By this time, Judith had joined them. "You can't find the cops arresting David anywhere, can you, Charley?"

"How did you know the cops were missing Judith?"

"There were six officers and the captain who went to arrest David. You got four dead here, so where are the others?"

"They'll turn up, Judith," Charley stated as he looked over the car where David had been. "Do you know how many officers were with the captain Officer Wilson?"

"There were six officers from our precinct, Charley, just like she said."

"So, who were the officers?" Charley continued to question. "If they were from our precinct, then the captain knows the names!"

"That's about the size of it, detective."

Never Die On A Cold Night II
<u>REVELATIONS</u>

"Where's the captain now?"

"You're not going over there, are you?" he asked.

Charley patted himself like he was patting a criminal, first upward on his chest and then down his thighs. Finally, his hands homed in on a slightly squared bulge in his pocket. He'd found his cigarettes. "What's it to you, Darren," he retorted as he pulled out the pack.

The officer was careful with his words now he'd noticed that Charley had changed from the usual mild-mannered individual to someone who seemed to be on the verge of going ballistic. He was aware of the temper of the man he was talking to after that bout with the captain. When Wilson spoke, he chose his words carefully. "Well, this case is a very important one, and I'm sure you want to stay on it. It might take someone who won't antagonize the captain and make him so defensive to get all the facts, don't you think?"

"All right, kid you've won the spot of mediator, so go get the information we need."

"Okay, detective," Wilson smiled. "I'll get right on it.

"Hey," Charley shouted, "you just make sure you get all the facts."

Officer Wilson smiled and nodded then walked to where the captain was sitting.

"Smart move," Judith said.

"You think so?" Charley said sarcastically.

"Yeah, I think so."

By
J. P. Leonard

Charley heard some commotion from the direction of the crowd. Judith heard it as well.

"Uh, the news people are here," Judith smiled. "What are you going to tell them?"

"I don't see why we have to tell them anything," Charley said. "The less they know, the better."

"I think they know much more than what you give them credit for, Charley." Just then, Jerry Lynch, a reporter who'd been at the scene of the Patricia Hill murder, was making his way through the crowd toward the first police car. Charley walked over to the reporter and stood between him and the police car. "I thought we'd gotten rid of you."

"You can't keep a good man down, detective." Jerry glanced over at Judith. "And aren't you going to introduce me, Charley?"

Charley shook his head, the nerve of this guy. "Special Agent for the FBI Judith O'Brian." Judith came closer to the two of them. Charley looked at her.

"Judith this is Jerry Lynch, a reporter for—"

"I know who he is."

"How do you know me? Have we met somewhere? No if we had I'd have remembered." Jerry stared at Judith for a while but turned his attention back to Charley. "You going to give me the story detective or do I have to work to get it?"

"Well, Jerry," Charley smiled now, "you know the drill."

"You guys think you have the public fooled, don't you?"

"What do you mean?" Charley asked.

Never Die On A Cold Night II
<u>REVELATIONS</u>

"There's a group going around—or shall I say gone underground calling itself the Red Pack. They've just about made a laughingstock of your police force. They've been everywhere you're supposed to be. You can't protect anybody from them, yet you don't want the public to know. I know it's the least of what you are hiding. There is something else you're hiding, something more sinister than any of us could ever imagine."

"What in the world are you talking about?" Charley asked again.

"Oh no, you're not going to get me this time Charley."

"What do you mean, little man? I think you better get out of here; I could care less about what you know," Charley said angrily.

"Hold on, Charley," Judith said. "I'd be interested to know what you're talking about off the record, of course."

"How about we talk about it over dinner?" Jerry asked.

"Sure, what time?" Judith smiled alluringly. "And where do I meet you?"

Jerry was completely surprised. "I have to work late tonight at the paper." Jerry's face and his neck were sweating, even in the cold. "I won't get off until ten thirty or maybe eleven."

Judith reached into her handbag and pulled out a card. "Why don't you just call me when you get done," Judith suggested with a smile.

"This is not a date, you know," Jerry said shyly. "I mean I'm not trying to get a date with you. It is only a business meeting."

"Whatever you say, Jerry," she responded.

"Well, this is all well and good," Charley said. "But I've got to get back to work."

Judith had successfully befuddled Jerry's attempts to get a story. It was obvious his mind was more on Judith than business because he just walked off without so much as a word.

"Well, I guess I helped you out of this one, Detective."

"So, why are you so nice to me, Judith?"

"I don't know. Maybe I shouldn't."

Charley looked her up and down with those once warm and friendly but now cold and suspicious eyes. He hated this woman, and he didn't understand why. For some reason, her beauty didn't move him. It wasn't because she was white or because she was an agent for the FBI. It wasn't even the great confidence in herself she possessed; after all, it could be a turn-on. No, it was something else. There was just something about the woman making him think she knew more about what was happening than anyone else. "So, what do you want, Judith?" Charley took out a small notepad and his pen and started to write into it.

"Do you want to find David?"

"Yeah." Charley looked up from his notepad. "I want to find him, and when I do, he's going to jail."

"Now, Charley, I thought you were on David's side." Judith walked closer to investigate his face. "When did you start believing he killed those women?"

Charley stuck the notepad back into his coat. "Judith, I would love to chitchat with you, but it's cold out here. I'm about to freeze my butt off so I'll see you back at the station."

"Okay, but I think it's very important we talk about this."

Charley had already started to walk away.

"Charley! Charley," she shouted. "We are going to have to talk about this."

Officer Wilson came back over. "Where is Charley? I got the information from the captain, and I also got something else from one of the dispatchers at the station; I guess it's not important."

"What is it, Officer?"

"You mean what the captain said?"

"No…" she said with a bit of annoyance in her voice. "What did dispatch say?"

"Well, the dispatcher said a kid called it in. The kid said someone told him to call it in."

"Did the kid say who it was?" Judith inquired of officer Wilson.

"It was a male."

"The kid said it was a man who told him."

"No, I'm saying the kid was a male."

"Officer Wilson." Judith was getting frustrated. "Who was it that told the kid to call in?" she asked, not bothering to hide her annoyance now.

"I tell you, ma'am; the kid sounded a little off. He said Superman told him to call. A handcuffed Superman. Ain't that a kick?"

"It was Detective Neal," she said as she scanned the crowd. "Maybe the child's still here."

"You know you're right it does sound like Detective Neal," Wilson conceded. "I guess. But do you think the child is still here? It's mighty cold out here."

"Look around and see if you find the kid in the crowd Officer Wilson. You take the crowd across the street, and I'll take the crowd right behind us."

Officer Wilson nodded and crossed over to the crowd to look for a child.

Almost convinced she wasn't going to find the kid, Judith walked slowly through the people; until she saw a little disabled black boy with a red cap. She smiled as she walked over to the boy.

The boy smiled back at her. "Are you a superhero, too?" the boy asked.

"No, I'm just an FBI agent," Judith responded.

"Oh." The boy sounded disappointed.

"But I like superheroes," Judith said.

That seemed to make the child feel better. "Superman was here," the disabled boy said as he pointed over to the wreckage. "He was fighting some bad people and some bad cops."

"Why do you think they were bad cops?"

The little boy hobbled around on his crutches to get a better position. "Because the Cops Superman was fighting started shooting into the last police car, and they were helping the bad men in the van chase, Superman."

"Did you see where they went?"

"Yeah. I followed the bad men and the bad police as fast as I could. These things do kind of slow me down some, but I was still able to keep up." he said, holding up his crutches.

"Can you take me where they went?"

"They're not there."

"Why did you say that?" Judith asked.

"Because they killed Superman and picked him up and put him in a black van."

"They killed him?" Judith's face was full of concern. "Are you sure they just didn't knock him out?"

The boy's face got serious. "You can't knock out Superman. I think the man must have used a kryptonite gun. It was a green kryptonite gun. The man shot Superman with it, and he just lay there."

"Did the gun make a loud noise?"

"No, ma'am, but the one he shot the old man with did."

"What, old man?"

"There was an old man who tried to hit Superman, but the bad policeman shot him with the loud gun then he shot Superman with the kryptonite gun."

"Did you happen to see the license plate number?"

"Yup, I wrote it down." The boy pulled out a folded-up piece of paper and gave it to Judith.

Judith beckoned to Officer Wilson and two other police officers on the scene.

Officer Wilson came first. "You found him?"

"Yes," she said. "The Red Pack has Detective Neal. I think they may have shot him with a tranquilizer gun."

"The Red Pack? How do you know?" Officer Wilson asked. At that point, the other officers had joined them.

"I want you all to go with us to where Detective Neal might have gone," Judith ordered.

"So, you will follow up on what the kid said?" Officer Wilson asked, shaking his head. "This kid doesn't know his head from a hole in the ground."

"Then you have a better idea, officer?"

"No, I just think it's a wild goose chase."

"What's your name, son?" Judith enquire.

"I don't like him," the boy said as he pointed to Officer Wilson.

"Don't worry about him; he worries about everything. Tell me your name," Judith softly demanded of the boy.

"My name's Jeffrey Belmont."

"My name's Judith O'Brian. Special Agent Judith O'Brian. Where are your parents, Jeffrey?"

"They're both dead."

Never Die On A Cold Night II
<u>REVELATIONS</u>

"I'm sorry, Jeffrey." Judith squatted down beside him and put her arm around him. "Who takes care of you now?"

"My grandmother. She's not too good at getting around, so I guess I kind of take care of her."

"I'll take you to where you live after you show me where the men were. Ok?

"Okay," the boy agreed.

Judith and the other officers followed the boy the same way he had followed David. When they got there, they saw nothing. "Is this where they were, Jeffrey?" Judith asked.

The boy had led them to the alley; the same alley Detective Neal had hurriedly entered. "Yes."

Officer Wilson looked around at the other police officers, and they all proceeded to the building David had entered. Officer Wilson went inside, and the other officers followed. Afterward, Wilson came out and beckoned to Judith, who had been standing a few yards away with the kid.

Judith and the kid started to walk over.

"You better let the kid stay outside," Officer Wilson said.

Judith looked down at Jeffrey. "Wait for me out here, ok?"

The boy looked at her and nodded.

Judith followed Darren inside the building to see what Darren and the other officers had found. It was the body of an old man. He still had a pipe in his hand that had blood and what seemed to be hair on it. Wilson called the homicide detectives in, and soon there were more uniformed police on scene as well. The captain showed up, as did Charley. Jerry Wilson, the deputy coroner was there also.

"So, did David do this?" the captain questioned.

"No, he didn't do this one either," Judith said as she put her arm around Jeffrey. "This child's name is Jeffrey. Jeffrey, this is Captain Edwards of the Chicago police department. Captain, he saw the whole thing."

The captain looked briefly at the child and then turned away to Charley. "I want the report on my desk first thing in the morning. We are being toyed with, it seems. At ten o'clock, we will have another meeting to assess where we are with all this," he commanded. He then turned to Judith. "And I want to know everything you know, or you get no further cooperation from my department or me." With that, the captain left.

Charley walked over to the deputy coroner and stooped down next to him over the body of the old man.

"It appears to be probably a forty-five that did it. I'll know more when I do the autopsy."

"Okay, Jerry," Charley said as he got up.

"You still don't believe the Red Pack captured him, do you, Charley?" Judith insisted.

"What difference does it make?" Charley responded. Nicola was found in David's room with his fingerprints all over the murder weapon, and I know she wouldn't have gone anywhere with him. Besides, we only have your word that the Red Pack even exists. No one is that powerful; it just doesn't jive."

"You know Charley," Judith posed, "you sound like you were kind of sweet on Nicola. I know how she was. Remember, she was my snitch. What you may not know is Nicola had a history of affairs with African American married men."

Charley looked at Judith with contempt.

"Anyway," she continued. "I believe the Red Pack framed him."

"You know, I believe your intentions are a little obvious," Charley said. "You are kind of sweet on David, but you are certainly not by yourself." Judith didn't say anything; she just continued to look at Charley. "Sadie Phillips is going to give you a run for your money." Judith kept her cool, or at least she seemed to. "Did you know when they picked him up, he was with Sadie?" Charley said, smiling.

"Yes, I know. David's a grown man. And the last time I heard; this was a free country. Charley, I don't think you ought to give up on your friend yet." Judith started to grin. "I mean, letting a tramp such as Nicola come between you, David just shouldn't be." Judith knew she had hit a nerve because she saw Charley starting to ball up his fist. She continued. "I mean, letting a thing like the male ego determine your friendship—the fact he might have been better in bed with Nicola than you were...."

Charley couldn't stand it anymore. He started toward Judith, but Jerry stood up between them.

"Judith, I think you better leave," Jerry said, looking at her with concern.

Judith only laughed. "I can certainly take care of myself." But she figured she'd done the damage she wanted to do, so she walked away. "See ya, Charley," she cracked as she walked away smiling.

By
J. P. Leonard

Jerry hung on to Charley, but the concerned look stayed on his face, not because of Charley and Judith, but from what he had learned from a previous case the department was working on. "Charley I've got to tell you about the Kelly girl I was going to do an autopsy on."

Charley was still steaming, so he didn't hear Jerry talking to him. A couple of Jerry's helpers came into the building with a body bag and a stretcher.

"Are you ready for us to pick up the body?" one of the men asked Jerry.

"Yes, I'm done here."

The men picked up the body and carried it out. The other people scouring the building for whatever evidence they might find were finally wrapping things up.

Charley, finally regaining his composure, allowed Jerry to continue.

"The body of the girl we placed in the morgue is gone," Jerry said. "Including all of the records and paperwork."

"Everything?"

"Everything."

Charley thought about it for a minute.

"Don't you think this is getting pretty crazy, Charley?" Jerry asked, looking around to see who was listening. "Who do we trust now? We can't seem to trust our own. I have never seen anything like this before. People are being killed right at the police station. Cops being snatched right out of our midst."

Never Die On A Cold Night II
<u>REVELATIONS</u>

"You don't know if that's true, Jerry," Charley said.

"Which part is untrue, the abduction of a cop or people dying in the police station or inability to trust our own?"

"David was not abducted. How could anyone with his skills get the best of him? The truth is I believe he killed those women."

"How can you say that? Detective David Neal is no murderer. You know he didn't kill anyone. I don't care what you said to that FBI agent. David wouldn't do anything of the kind."

"You know, I was David's friend. If anybody knows him, I do."

"So, then, why are you looking to hang him? Charley this isn't like you."

"We're through here," one of Charley's team said as he walked up to Charley and Jerry. "You want us to do anything else, detective?"

"No, we can pack it up."

Jerry asked the men working with Charley. "What did you guys find?"

"Isn't that out of your bounds of authority?" Charley was starting to get angry.

"I don't think so; I'm allowed to access whatever information is available to determine how a murder was committed and the circumstances surrounding it. It's my job. Now, are you going to stop me from doing my job?"

Charley grinned at Jerry. "No, I'm not going to stop you. Get all the information you need."

So, Jerry turned to the man standing there. "So, did you find that there were others here?"

"There were several other people here. They seemed to have been fighting from the looks of things. There was a broken mop by the steps, and it appeared someone fell on it and broke it. Looking at the shoe prints on the floor, they had to be fighting."

"Charley, the pipe the old man had in his hands had blood on it," Jerry said, directing his attention back to Charley. "This is all consistent with what the little boy was saying."

"You're probably right, Jerry, but explain the murdered hotel owner and the murder of Nicola."

Jerry paused. "I don't know, Charley, I don't know. But I still can't figure out David as being the murderer."

"Facts are facts."

"Is that all, detective?" the team member asked again.

"Are you finished, Jerry?" Charley said.

Jerry looked around the area again where the old man's body had been. His mind failed to come up with any more questions or answers. "Yeah, sure, let's get out of here."

"Okay," Charley happy to agree. "I think we can all go now."

C H A P T E R   T W O

"Secrets to reveal"

David had wakened from the deep sleep which the injection from the dart had placed him. When he opened his eyes, he found himself wishing he could have stayed in a deep sleep forever. He realized he had awakened back into the nightmare he had been compelled to exist in some time before. He was in that dungeon of a cell again. His old companions were also there. Maybe some of the same rats which had so graciously avoided him before were now stuck with him again. At least it seemed to be the same ones just as before, which would not come near him. He began to remember everything. It all came back to him in a flood.

Why were they willing to spare his life? They had already framed him, so what more did they want? Just then, a bright light seemed to come from nowhere and started illuminating a corner of the room adjacent to his position on the floor. He couldn't move very fast; he wanted to raise his hand to his eyes to wipe them, thinking maybe his eyes were playing tricks on him again as before. Then he saw her; it was the same woman he'd seen before. She was looking at him with tearful eyes. Who was she? Then she spoke to him.

"Help him, David, please help him. He's going to die."

"What do you mean help him? Help who?" David asked her. He tried to get up, but he didn't seem to have the strength.

"Help him, David, he's going to die." And with that, she disappeared, and it was dark again.

Was he losing his mind? He didn't know. It must have been the drug they shot into him. Maybe that was the reason he'd seen the woman this time but what about the other times? His strength seemed to return. He got to his feet and went over to the door. He pushed it gently, and it gave a little. He continued to push on the door, and it opened all the way. He looked around and again just as before the scenery was the same. There were electric lights so many feet apart down the wall until it got to the stairs. Everything was the same. Only this time he didn't think he'd been there long. Other than the slight grogginess from the drug he felt strong. This time he raced down the hall to the stairs. He had to see what was in store for him. Would it be as the last time or would he step into something more bizarre than he had dreamed before?

At the same time in another building housing a huge newspaper company in Chicago on the fifth floor for the educational enlightenment and amusement of the public sat Jerry Lynch at his desk.

"Mista Lynch suh," an older African American man with a dust mop in hand, wearily approached a busy Jerry Lynch. He was trying to get Jerry's attention. "You gonna be very long?"

"Just a few minutes, Conroy I'll just be a feeew more minutes."

"You know how Mista Jameson likes all the lights out at this time. I gotta turn the ceiling light out, Ok?" he asked as he waited for a reaction.

Jerry typed a few more words of the paragraph he was writing and stopped momentarily. He turned to the man standing behind him. "I'm sorry, Conroy. I know you're trying to do your job, but I've got to get this finished. I tell you what; go ahead. Clean around me and turn out the overhead light. I think I'll be able to see. I got to make a phone call anyway, so go ahead and turn the light out."

"Thanks, Mista Lynch."

"'Ok, Conroy," Jerry said as he turned himself around. "Have a good night now."

"You too, Suh," the old man smiled.

Jerry picked up the receiver of the phone in front of him and hesitated for a few seconds and hung the phone back up. "I can't do it," he said out loud. "That FBI agent had to be pulling my leg; she doesn't want me." For a minute, he just looked at the phone. Then just as the lights went out the phone rang and he jumped so hard he hit his knee on the underside of the desk. He swore out loud as he reached for the receiver. "City desk Jerry speaking can I help you?" he asked nursing his sore knee.

"Hello, Jerry," a sexy woman's voice answered on the other end. "Did you forget our date?"

"Judith, is that you?"

"Were you expecting someone else?"

"I didn't—no—I mean yes I mean I was going to call you. I kind of got a little tied up."

"Would you rather we did this another time?" she teased.

"Yes, I mean no. I mean we can still do this. I am just about finished."

"Okay then I'll pick you up there," Judith said. "Is that all right?"

"Yeah sure. I'll hurry and get this done."

"Don't hurry. It will probably take me about thirty minutes to get there ok?"

"All right. I'll be downstairs when you get here."

"O.k. bye, Jerry."

"Good-bye, Judith I'll see you in thirty minutes." Jerry hadn't been with anybody since high school. He seemed to have been more popular then. He was slim and trim muscular with not an ounce of fat on his body at the age of seventeen. He had been into sports that year wrestling, and running track were his specialties. Now—the years had caught up with him. No one would recognize him inside the fat body he possessed today. He smiled when he remembered the day he'd had two girls wanting to fight each other over him. Deborah had given him a ring and Sharon had given him a scarf. One day Sharon saw him wearing the scarf around his neck with the ring Deborah had given him holding it together and asked him if she could wear the scarf and the ring, so he said ok and gave it to her. Later that day Deborah saw the ring around Sharon's neck and without warning the fight was about to start. Some of the people around had prevented the fight from happening. When the news got around the school—he became one of the most popular guys on the campus.

This date with Judith brought back some fond memories. Maybe he might get it all back thinking he could start to work out again. He reached over and picked up a small mirror from off his desk, that he sometimes used for shaving. Sometimes when he had been so in a hurry to check out a story, he not only wouldn't shave but sometimes he hadn't washed. It seemed to happen a lot lately. He wondered if he smelled okay. He sniffed up under one arm and then the other. He couldn't tell if he smelled or not. Looking into the mirror, he decided the story could wait—he'd have to go wash up. There was one thing he worried about though he could wash his body and maybe smell better but, what in the world was he going to do about his face the years had not been kind he was one ugly sucker. Well—anyway—Judith didn't seem to mind his pus, and he could wash up in the men's room. He still had all those important papers and taped interviews and reports on computer disks right in front of him. Every piece of evidence on the bizarre murders was lying in a pile on his desk. Any other time he would have put the stuff in his desk and locked it up, but today he decided not to. Nobody was there but him and the old man, Conroy, besides he was coming right back. He left his desk and went outside to the men's room.

Later Conroy had just got around to the men's room when he saw Mr. Lynch go in. He liked Mr. Lynch because he wasn't like a lot of people there at the paper. People who looked down their noses at him. Funny he thought, he had been working there a long time and he still wasn't used to the fact people didn't respect him just because he was a man of color and a janitor. There was nothing else he could do he had worked all his life. He had to quit school when his father died. His mother needed help with raising and taking care of the other children. His father had been good to them but unrealistic to think he could care for thirteen children working for peanuts at a restaurant as a dishwasher. He thought to himself they did seem to manage though until his father died. After that, it seemed impossible to keep things together.

As Conroy thought about these things, he continued to mop the floor until he was ready to pull the mop bucket outside of the office. When he pulled the metal pail of mop water out of the office into the hall, he thought he heard something. Where did the sound come from, he wondered? Then just a few doors down in the washroom he had seen Mr. Lynch go into he heard another sound like something hitting something metal. A few seconds later he heard a loud thud against the bathroom door. In the next moment, he heard the most blood-curdling scream he had ever heard in all his life. It made him freeze in his tracks. Somehow, he knew the scream belonged to Mr. Lynch. He just stood in the middle of the hall floor shaking. He had never been so afraid in his life. The next few moments might prove to be his last. Something inside his mind was screaming at him to run using all the speed and power he could muster. But fear gripped him like a huge vice and simultaneously stripped his ability to control the motor functions via his brain to his legs. Before he realized it, he had moved down the hall and placed himself right outside the door. Panic-stricken he managed to knock on the door ever so lightly and softly call, "M-M-Mista L-L-Lynch," as if he didn't want to hear an answer from anyone or anything on the other side of the door.

Conroy could hear nothing there was only silence. The blood was rushing through his body with every thump his heart made. He hadn't even realized pain was starting to shoot all the way from his back down his left arm to his fingertips until he noticed he couldn't breathe. What, at a time like this? How could he have a heart attack? Conroy felt as if a thousand-pound weight pressed on his chest. He tried to play it off, but he knew he was having a heart attack. At least he was comforted knowing he wouldn't have to experience whatever Mr. Lynch was experiencing. All of the murders happening he knew no sane person could ever be responsible for such inhuman acts.

Conroy felt himself falling to the floor as the door in front him burst apart splintering into a million pieces and sending him flying into the wall opposite the bathroom. As his head hit the wall, it might have knocked him unconscious if it was not for the fact before his head hit, he was already dead.

By
J. P. Leonard

By
J. P. Leonard

CHAPTER THREE

"No news is bad news."

About fifteen minutes later, Judith O'Brian was knocking on the main entry doors of the Daily News Building. A lone watchman sitting in his round information booth was looking at a nudie magazine when the knocking made him look at the small tv screen on his desk. Hurriedly he pressed the button that activated the intercom speakers on the outside. "What can I do for you, ma'am?" the watchman said in the smoothest voice he could muster.

"Hello, I'm looking for a Mr. Jerry Lynch," she said, smiling into the camera she saw just above her head.

"Hold on, miss; I'll call up to see if he's available."

"I'm sure he is, sir, but do you think I can come in from the cold? It's freezing out here."

The man looked at the phone and hesitated for a moment.

Never Die On A Cold Night II
<u>REVELATIONS</u>

"Yeah, sure, I guess it'll be all right. I'll be right there."

Judith watched the man come down the hall; he was grinning from ear to ear. She noticed he was a big and quite handsome guy. He must have been about twenty-five to thirty years old. She could see the muscles bulging through his shirt and figured he must spend a lot of time at the gym somewhere. Unlocking the door, she watched his eyes; they were all over her body as his hands would have been if she had allowed him it. No matter how good he looked, he was not a David Neal. Besides, she needed to keep her mind on the situation at hand.

"I haven't seen you here before," he said softly. "I would have remembered somebody as beautiful as you."

"I hope you don't think a line like that turns me on," she said as she raised her eyebrow.

"I would never try to insult you this way," he said very sincerely. "However, I am guilty of being outspoken. I tend to speak what's on my mind."

"Look, why don't you just call Jerry and leave it at that?"

"All right, but if you change your mind, you know where I am."

As they made it up to the information booth, the watchman began to call Jerry's floor. No one answered. He called out to Jerry and then to the janitor but got no one. He had no way of knowing the terrible fate that had befallen the two. The watchman was trying to impress Judith by showing his efficiency, but no one was cooperating. Now he was beginning to get annoyed. Someone was supposed to call back. Was the equipment not working?

"Is something wrong?" Judith said, looking at the man with

pitiful eyes.

"No, it's okay," the man said. "They both might be in the john."

"Both of them—at the same time?" She smiled.

"Doesn't seem likely, does it?" The watchman was starting to look desperate. He then decided to use the public-address system instead of the private intercom. "Jerry Lynch, please call down to the information desk," he said, his voice now booming all over the building. He waited thirty seconds and then called the janitor. "Conroy, please call the desk." He waited thirty more seconds, but no response came.

"Could anyone have left without you knowing about it?" Judith asked him.

"Absolutely not. I'm going to have to check this out," he said, coming out of the information booth. "Uh, please stay here, Miss. I'll—"

Judith interrupted him as she took out her badge. "That's all right. I'm an FBI agent. Let's go on up together."

"Hey, I'm in charge of this place here, and I say wait downstairs."

Judith looked down at the floor and then walked closer to him while looking into his eyes. "Now look, mister, I know you feel you're doing your job, but I represent an official government agency. I do have some powers you might not think I have, such as having the I.R.S. to go over certain tax returns at a moment's notice."

"I don't have anything to hide. Let them come," the watchman said defiantly.

Never Die On A Cold Night II
<u>REVELATIONS</u>

"Even if they come every month for a year," Judith said, smiling.

"You wouldn't do that."

"Worse things have happened," Judith replied as she held the badge up.

The watchman looked at the badge, then at her, and decided he'd better cooperate. They went upstairs together. When they got up to the floor, it was dark. He found a light switch and turned it on. Judith followed the watchman to the room Jerry had been working in and found the lamp that had been on his desk on the floor. Papers were all over the floor. As they got closer to the scene, they could see the vandalized computer.

"What happened here?" the watchman asked.

"Are you sure no one else is up here?"

"Sure, I'm sure. No one could have gotten past me, but..."

"What?" Judith asked.

He looked at her. "There could have been someone here before I came on duty. Someone could have easily stayed in the building after it was locked up. I checked all the doors upstairs and downstairs, and they were secure. I don't understand."

They walked around the hall until they got to the restrooms. Judith held out her arm instinctively to slow down the watchman, and at the same time she pulled out her weapon. "Someone could still be up here." The light was out down the hall, and they couldn't see very well.

"There is a light switch on this wall over here," the watchman said, crossing over to it. He tried the switch, and nothing happened. "Do you feel that?" he asked Judith.

"Do I feel what?"

"A draft of cold air. It's always warm up here," he said.

"Now that you mention it, I do feel a cold draft coming from somewhere. What's down here?"

"A couple of offices and the men's room."

"Well, let's check it out but be careful," she said.

As they got closer to the bathroom, the watchman saw the janitor. "Oh my God, it looks like Conroy," he said as he ran down to the janitor. "What is this all over the floor?" Judith was right behind him. "Watch yourself," he said. "There is something all over the floor—it looks like wood." They were right in front of a dark and doorless men's room. "The door is gone," the watchman said. "Who or what could have done this?"

Judith knelt beside the old man and felt for his pulse. "He's dead!"

"You sound surprised."

"He just could have appeared dead. I thought he might still be alive. You better call for an ambulance anyway."

"What about Jerry? He's got to be up here as well?" he said.

"I'll look for Jerry. You go and call the police and an ambulance."

The watchman ran back to Jerry's office and called the police. A few minutes later, he ran back down to where Judith was, and he saw her looking inside the bathroom.

Never Die On A Cold Night II
REVELATIONS

"Listen, Jerry is in there but don't go in."

"Why?" He tried to see what she had seen, but it was dark. Where the window was supposed to be, there was nothing but a dark blue sky lit by the light of a full moon.

"The guy must have gone back through the window," Judith said.

"I don't think so," the watchman replied. "It's a five-story drop all the way down. But I don't see Jerry. Is he alive?"

"He's dead. He's shredded like a piece of paper. To go in there now would contaminate the scene," Judith answered him.

"Poor Conroy," the man said, looking at the old man again. He then turned back to the bathroom, squinting his eyes in the dark. "I can't see a thing."

Judith looked up and around the ceiling. "There has got to be a light switch somewhere that should turn these lights on."

"I'd forgotten there is an emergency master switch, mainly, I guess because I never had to use it. It will turn on the emergency lights on this floor." At least, that's what the watchman figured.

"On your way to wherever the switch is, you might want to let the police in when they get here," she said.

The watchman went down into the lobby and through one of the doors leading to the basement. He tried a light switch at the basement door, but it had no effect. As he went downstairs to the basement, he noticed a flashlight hanging on the wall. He stood for a moment and turned on the flashlight. He thought to himself as he shined the light on the dark; this place gives me the willies. Soon he found the control box for all the lights in the building. As he looked into the box, all the breakers were on except one.

By
J. P. Leonard

That was the breaker carrying all the lights for all the bathrooms and the basement where he was. The basement was flooded with light after the watchman flipped the switch. While he was pondering the idea, he heard a banging upstairs. Walking upstairs, he headed down the hall. He noticed a door to one of the offices was opened. It hadn't been open before. He had checked. He went to the door and opened it further, shining his light into the darkness. Suddenly someone ran out from the shadows and dived into him before he had a chance to react. Back they went into the wall. The guy was almost as big as he was. The attacker got up first and began to run in the direction of the double doors. The watchman got to his feet almost immediately, picking up the flashlight he had dropped in the scuffle. He began to chase the fleeing attacker. He noticed the guy had started to run to the doors but then changed his direction and started to run up the stairs. The attacker had seen the police outside banging on the door and decided he'd find another way out.

The police outside started to bang on the door again. The watchman started to run after the guy but decided to let the police in first. As he opened the door, Officer Darren Wilson was the first to come through with his gun drawn.

"Who are you?" he asked the watchman.

"I'm Michael Lewis, the night watchman."

Wilson looked at the ID badge on the watchman's shirt. "Who were you just chasing?" Darren asked.

"I think he could have been the murderer."

"Was he armed?"

"I don't know."

Never Die On A Cold Night II
REVELATIONS

Officer Wilson looked at the other four policemen with him, "Let's go."

Judith had heard the banging on the door as she was coming down the stairs and figured the police were outside. She was surprised to see the man coming straight at her up the stairs. The man was running and looking back down the steps, so he didn't see her. Judith dropped her purse and started running down the steps toward the man. Before the man had time to react, Judith sidestepped him grabbed his arm, and twisted downward, and his momentum caused his body to flip. The man landed hard on his back on the metal steps. He was temporarily dazed; this gave Judith time to roll him over and handcuff him before Officer Wilson made it up the steps.

"Judith—you okay?" Officer Wilson asked as he came up the stairs.

"Yeah, I'm fine, but I don't know about him."

"What happened? We got a call that someone had been murdered. We were waiting at the lobby door when this character came running around the corner. Do you think he could be a suspect?" Darren asked.

"I don't know, Darren. Maybe! On the fifth floor in the men's room," she said, smoothing her hair. "There are two dead bodies in all."

"If he's not a suspect, whom do you think he is?" Darren asked as he motioned the officers up the stairs. "He reminds me of one of those biker types. Look at him—beard, bandana, leather clothes."

"I don't think he's riding a bike—in all that snow," Judith said as she ran her hands through her long, amber-colored hair. "We'll have to ask him who he is. As I said, he may be a suspect."

By
J. P. Leonard

"Do you mean a suspect in the murders in this building?"

"One murder Officer Wilson just one murder. I'm not sure what happened to the old man upstairs, but I am certain Jerry's murder was by the same person or persons we've been after."

"You think this guy could have done it, Judith?"

"I don't know about that. He may know something, though."

The man began to stir.

"I'm going back upstairs, Officer Wilson. Can you handle him?"

"Yeah, I can handle him," the young officer said as he started to pick the man up.

"Hold it; we've got one more." It was Charley coming up the stairs with a young girl. She looked to be around twenty-one or twenty-two and very pretty. She had on leather as well. "She says she's with him."

When the girl saw her boyfriend on the steps, she went hysterical. She screamed at the top of her lungs while trying to get away from Charley. "You didn't have to kill him."

Judith went down to the girl and grabbed her by the arm, pulling her up the stairs to bring her closer to her boyfriend. She pulled her so hard that the girl almost tripped. "Look," she said to the girl. "There is nothing wrong with him."

By that time, Officer Wilson had pulled him to his feet. The girl quieted down.

"What were you two doing in here?" Judith asked the two of them.

Never Die On A Cold Night II
REVELATIONS

"Nothing," the handcuffed man said.

 One officer came down, and Charley went up to him and whispered something to the cop. The officer left the group of them and went downstairs.

"So, you were doing nothing. Then why did you run from the security guard?" Judith said, continuing to grill them.

"We didn't do anything. We just came in to get out of the cold," the man said.

"Honest, Miss," the girl said. "We just wanted to be warm. But there was—"

The guy with her cut her off. "Shut up, Darlene."

"Wait a minute, buddy, let the young lady talk," Charley said. "If you want to get out of here, you had better cooperate with us."

Judith asked the woman softly. "What did you want to say, Darlene? Remember, no one is going to hurt you. Did you see anything out of the ordinary?"

"No, I didn't see anything."

The group did not say anything for a while. It was evident the young man and his girlfriend knew more than they were telling.

"Darren, take these two downstairs and keep them there until we get some answers," Charley told the officer.

"You're not going to let us go?" the young girl asked.

"Not until you decide to cooperate with us," Judith replied. she turned her back to the girl as Officer Wilson escorted them downstairs.

36

By
J. P. Leonard

Charley took his topcoat off and placed it on his arm.

"You're looking pretty spiffy tonight. What's the occasion? Is that a new suit?" Judith asked.

"Yeah, I bought it today," Charley told her as he looked at her sideways.

"It looks good." Judith smiled. "It makes you look good, Charley."

"I guess I'm supposed to thank you for the compliment."

"Charley," she said. "I'm not looking for anything. It was an honest and sincere compliment. So, what's the occasion."

"Janet and I went out for a while. We had just got back when I got the call. So, what do we have, Judith?"

"It's up on the fifth floor. A murder just like the others."

They started to walk up the stairs.

"I was told there were two of them?" Charley asked, waiting for a reply.

"I don't know. There is an old man, but there aren't any visible reasons for his death. But Jerry Lynch's death is the same as all the others."

"Jerry Lynch?" Charley said, visibly surprised. "The newspaper guy, the one you were supposed to go out with?"

"That's the one."

"So, you hated your date that much?"

Judith just looked at him. "What are you saying, Charley?"

she asked as they made it to the second floor.

"I was kidding. Can't you take a joke?" he said, smiling.

"You never joke with your partner like that, " she said seriously.

"Sure, sure. It's just that when PMS kicks in, you never know what you women might do." Charley smiled.

"Charley," she said, smacking him on the arm. "That's not fair."

Charley looked up the rest of the stairs. "Don't they have an elevator in this building?"

"You getting soft in your old age, Charley? I'll bet at one time you could have run up and down these stairs ten times without breathing hard."

"Yeah, probably a long time ago."

"You don't work out anymore?"

"As little as possible. My wife does, and she tried to get me to go, but I was always too busy. Her and my daughter...." Charley stopped walking and looked down at the steps.

"I'm sorry about your daughter Charley. I truly am," Judith said. "'We have got to get these guys."

Charley looked at Judith. "What is it about you, Judith? Why are you really helping us to get these people; that is if they really exist? What is your angle? What do you get out of all this?"

Judith continued up the stairs, and Charley followed. "Maybe I'll tell you someday, Charley. I do have my reasons."

"You have to understand, Judith," Charley continued. "In the past, whenever the department has tried to work with the FBI, it has always proved to have been worse than pulling hen's teeth!"

"Hens don't have teeth, Charley." Judith kept climbing the stairs.

"You don't say?"

"So, what's your point, Charley?"

"The FBI always seem to have their own agenda, whether we've worked with them or not. They usually never give us the whole story, and here you are, giving us whatever information, we desire. Well, it just doesn't add up."

"Look at it like a godsend Charley. If you were starving, you wouldn't beat the cook up for bringing you the dinner, would you? You'd eat it and be happy. Take what I give you and be happy."

They finally made it to the top of the stairs, where the police had already put up the yellow caution tape. They had to duck under it to get by.

"I hope nobody moved anything," Judith said to the uniformed officers. She looked at her watch. "What's keeping my team?"

"I don't think they're coming yet," Charley replied.

"How do you know?"

"Well, I told the dispatcher not to call them yet."

"Why?" Judith asked, with a confused look on her face. "We're supposed to work together, aren't we?"

Never Die On A Cold Night II
<u>REVELATIONS</u>

"Calm down; they'll come. I just wanted to get Jerry Wilson over here first."

"Now you know we have the best possible equipment to do the job. You don't have the technology we have. Wait a minute. Oh, I see. You don't trust us, do you?"

"What do you think I've been trying to tell you?" When they got to the bathroom, Charley was about to go in.

"There is blood all over the place, Charley, so watch your step. So, what can I do to make you trust me?"

"I don't know, Judith. Time, I guess. Give me time."

"Time is a luxury I can't afford to give."

"So be it, Judith. Then we'll have to agree to disagree. Now let's get to work."

Judith stared at him for a while, then began to brief him. "As you can see Charley it's the same as the Piece-of-cake murder. The body is shredded all except the head, and there is no blood on it."

The deputy coroner gave no thought to the fact there were two people in the building viewed as possible suspects. He knew they had no means to kill the way those people had been killed. Who or what had killed Piece-of-cake and the others was a mystery to him The question was how it could be done so quickly. The most baffling one of all was the Kelly murder. The time it took for death to occur the way it did was as unlikely as what had caused the death. Now here was another murder just as puzzling as the others.

"There he is now," Judith told Charley.

"I'll talk to you later Judith," Charley said as he put on his coat and walked past Jerry Wilson without speaking to or acknowledging him. Jerry watched him leave the scene and then proceeded to where the bodies were.

"Gee this is a mess," Jerry said as he viewed the body of Jerry Lynch. Looking across to the old man he walked over and knelt beside him. The body was leaning against the wall like he was sitting there sleeping. "Well old man what happened to you?" Jerry said. Then he noticed Judith standing there. "Oh, hi Judith how's tricks?"

"Tricks? That's not a cordial thing to ask a lady," Judith replied.

"I'm sorry, how have you been since I saw you last."

"Not too good."

"Anything I can do to help?" Jerry asked.

"Actually you're helping me now. Helping me to catch the men who are responsible for these murders is help enough," Judith smiled.

"I'm not so sure if the men you are looking for are responsible for all of the murders Judith."

Judith's interest was piqued by what Jerry had just said. "So, who do you think did them?"

"Your guess is as good as mine. What have you produced?" he asked.

"Not a lot but we do know the Red Pack is involved in sacrificing and voodoo and supposedly worshipping of demons. Which leaves us to determine that the murders were the results of human sacrifices."

"Then how do you explain the bites with nonhuman saliva in them?" Jerry said as he stood up.

"Are you serious, Jerry? We thought the saliva traces weren't identified. The next thing you will say is that the murderer wasn't human."

Jerry didn't say anything. He just walked over to the body of Jerry Lynch. "What human is capable of that?" he said, pointing to the shredded body of Jerry Lynch.

"I think you are reading too much into this, Jerry," Judith said with a chuckle. "You're talking about things that don't exist except in late-night horror movies. I'll tell you what, though, if you have any real proof of these allegations, I'll be more than happy to listen." Judith looked at her watch again. "Where are my guys? I'm going to have to call them. Look, Jerry, I'm going to make a telephone call to get my guys here. I need to know what you find O.K."

"All right, Judith, I'll be right here."

By
J. P. Leonard

CHAPTER FOUR

"Secrets to reveal"

Back in the strange building with its dungeons and its great
rooms, a weary David Neal had entered the great room where the
food and servants had been before, only to find the room dark
and empty and no way out. His mind was racing. He had to find
a way out. "I don't understand this," he said out loud. "What do
these people want from me?" David moved slowly through the
darkness, and as he did, he could make out some shadows and
shapes in the room, having been there before. The shapes and
shadows helped him to be able to picture what was there. "C'mon
out and show yourself," he shouted. "Why are you doing this? If
this is supposed to be a torture treatment or some mind game, you
have missed the boat. You might as well show yourselves and
stop wasting my time."

Then a very deep voice began to speak to him. "Welcome to
my humble abode Detective David Neal."

"It's about time. Do you realize what you did? You have
kidnapped a police officer."

Never Die On A Cold Night II
<u>REVELATIONS</u>

There was silence for a minute.

"I don't think anyone else believes that David. Including your partner Charley."

"Who are you?" David asked.

"I'm the one you've been looking for."

"Francisco Hanniz, what an unpleasant surprise," David mocked the voice. The voice was coming from everywhere. Hanniz must have speakers all over the room. He still could not find a door that would lead him out.

"It's no use, David; there is no way out for you at this time," the voice said.

"What do you want?"

"What do I want? I don't want anything. Everything I want, I already have. No, it's not what I want but maybe what you want."

"And what do I want?"

"For one thing, David, I know you want your freedom. Isn't that right?"

"Go on."

"But how can you get your freedom when the police are after you, David?"

"You killed those people, Hanniz."

"That's not what the police believe. Your captain wants to hang you out to dry. Your partner believes you stole his girl. He wants to lock you up as well."

"How do you know all this?"

"It is my business to know."

"Who are you, really? You must have spies in our department.

"There is a lot you don't know, David. For one thing, I did not kill anyone in your police department or have anyone killed in your police department. As I said before, and I say again, there is a lot you don't know."

David knew there had to be more to the murders where the bodies were shredded the way they were, but he just didn't want to believe it. It was too fantastic to think of some monster walking around killing people in Chicago like in the dreams he was having. So, he deflected himself from those thoughts and focused on the monster talking to him instead. "I know you were responsible for the killing of Patricia Hills, the hotel owner, and the murder of Nicola."

"Yes, I admit that, but it was either them or let them kill you."

"I don't believe you, Hanniz. Why would Patricia Hills, someone I just met, want to kill me? I was protecting Nicola. Why would she want to kill me?"

"The competition, my competition. Your government is doing more than they are letting on. There is more corruption in your government than you realize."

"Look, Hanniz, you may be right about my government looking out for their interest, but why would they want to kill me?"

"You know too much, David."

"What I do know is I don't know anything," David stated.

Never Die On A Cold Night II
<u>REVELATIONS</u>

"O.K., I'll play along—what is it I'm supposed to know?"

"David, I am in a much better position than you are. I am privy to more information than you ever knew existed. Mistakes were made by your government while you were in special forces in Vietnam fighting the good fight. Your government made deals amongst themselves to cover those mistakes and to cover their behinds. You were told to do one job which was highly classified. You were told in the year 1972 to take your team of men and infiltrate the enemy headquarters east of your position and utterly-destroy everyone there. You were told later the target was a mistake, and that you had killed innocent men, women, and children. There was a big cover-up, and you resigned believing you alone made the mistake."

David was flabbergasted. "How did you get that kind of information unless…you have a part in our government. The information was highly classified. To save us embarrassment at-a-later date everything was redacted; nothing was left uncovered."

"You're right. To the point, it was a part of the deal for the United States to pull out of Vietnam so none of this would ever be made public. What you did not know is that the target was not a mistake. The extermination of all those people in that village was meant to be. The Vietnamese government wanted it as well as the United States. Don't you realize if the United States acted alone it would have been revealed? The problem was when the U.S. was supposed to be working with the South Vietnamese, they were working with the North which is why they pulled out. They collaborated with the North to destroy that village. Which is also highly classified."

David couldn't believe Hanniz had that kind of information.

"David you are in danger, and unless you let us help you, you will die," the voice said.

Then David remembered where he had heard the voice. It was in the dream he'd had.

"David, I am going to let you think about this for a while. Sorry about the accommodations but if you were in my position, you'd do the same thing."

David felt something hit his thigh, and a sharp pain penetrated his skin and total darkness again flooded his consciousness.

The next morning at the Twenty-Third Precinct the police briefing room was filled-to-capacity. Present were the FBI the police captains from the Third, Twenty-third and the Nineteenth precinct plus a hundred or so police from all three precincts and the mayor who was presiding over the whole meeting.

The Mayor stood up to speak. "What is it that we know ladies and gentlemen? I'll tell you. The federal government is about to take over our town because they think we are too incompetent to handle our own business."

The head of the FBI in the Illinois region stood up. "It's not a matter of the government believing you are incompetent," he said. "We have the resources and workforce unavailable to you. We have authority and jurisdiction over the whole U.S., and you don't. It's not a matter of us taking over. We're trying to help because we believe this case and the people involved will overwhelm your resources and personnel."

The Mayor looked at the man and then shook his head. "At this point, I am forced to have to cooperate with you but let me go on record I don't trust you at all. Information is something you people specialize in, and I'm sure you people know more than what you are telling us. I don't trust you, people, as far as I could throw an elephant. However, upon the express command of the governor of Illinois, this case has now been placed under the jurisdiction of the Federal Bureau of Investigations. So, I now put you in the hands of Thomas Fitzgerald Deputy Assistant Director of the FBI. He oversees this investigation now."

D.A.D. Fitzgerald stood up and introduced himself. He was a direct, no-nonsense former military man. Everything he said he meant. He was the head of covert operations in Vietnam which later landed him a job with the Federal Bureau of Investigation. Wanted by every intelligence agency in the United States, Fitzgerald had offers from other countries as well. When he was assigned to a mission, he successfully completed them. He was a very intelligent man. He appeared to be no more than fifty, but he was sixty-three years old and had been in great physical condition. He had run the whole FBI until a couple of years ago. He went dark for some unknown reason which is to say he stayed in the background and most never knew why? He was now only available for special jobs. He never worked in the field, but all assignments were completed successfully. He had gained a considerable amount of weight since the last time anyone had seen him. It seemed each time he made an appearance he was heavier but, this ruggedly handsome old man was still as dignified and authoritative as he'd always been. In the military, he'd learned to walk tall and be straight as an arrow mentally and physically. He was a serious man a man who never seemed to smile. All the men under his commands called him Old Iron Face because they'd never seen him smile but they trusted him as they might trust a parent. When he spoke, people paid attention, to his very deep raspy voice." I realize you people have already put more hours into this case than you would have liked. You are good people and determined to do your job. However, I am bringing you a fresh approach to bringing down the people responsible for all of these murders which have recently plagued your city. I know you have not seen your families for weeks. So, before you continue, I am going to give you two days to see them." All eyes were now fixed firmly on D.A.D. Fitzgerald. "That's right. I need my people to be alert. We will catch these murderers. Don't worry I promise you this. So, we will meet back here—unless we are forced to meet sooner—in two days. Today is Monday that means Wednesday at nine a.m. we will meet back here. However, I want to meet with Detective Stilles, Special Agent O'Brian, Officer Wilson, and Officer Delfonso. Otherwise, you are all dismissed."

After the meeting dismissed, five people remained in the conference room. "We don't get any time off," D.A.D. Fitzgerald stated. "I have found the people in charge to set the stage. Everybody else will follow the leader. The more focused and prepared you are the smoother this operation will go. Now I want on my desk a complete report of what has happened since this case first started no later than three o'clock today. I want all the information you have at the specified time I have given you. No excuses. Anyone bringing excuses doesn't work for me. I want you two officers with Detective Stilles at all times."

Charley was becoming visibly annoyed. "I can take care of myself. I don't need a nursemaid."

"I realize that, Charley but we need some bait, and it appears you're it. Now you are going to cooperate, or you are out, and you are still bait. Either way will suit me."

Charley had never met a man like the D.A.D. He decided to comply to see where the old man was going. "Don't worry about me I'm in," Charley replied as he sat back in his chair.

"Good man. I knew we could count on you Charley," The D.A.D. said in his deep, rasping voice. "For the next couple of days, I am going to work from the headquarters of the Third Precinct. Afterward, you won't know where I am, but I will be in constant contact with you. No one will do anything without express permission from me. We will work as a team. All information will go through me. Special Agent O'Brian I will take command of the mobile command center. You will continue as before, but in a different location with your men. I will use my own. Any questions?"

No one had any questions so the meeting was adjourned.

Judith left to prepare to move her equipment. When she got to the mobile command center, she found not her men but the D.A.D's. As she stepped on to the truck, she immediately had an escort of two women dressed in army fatigues.

"Right this way ma'am," one of the two said to her. Both women were Africa American, and they looked identical to one another. They both looked like bodybuilders and not very feminine.

"I need some of those records there," Judith said as she started over to the command booth.

"No ma'am all you need are in these boxes," one of the twins said pointing to about ten or eleven large boxes sitting on the floor in the corner of the room."

"What about my things?" Judith asked.

"Everything is in the boxes ma'am," one of them said.

"Well, I think I had better see for myself," Judith said as she tried to walk past one of the women but before she could her path was blocked. "If you don't get out of my way, I'm going to make a doorway right through you."

"Please ma'am I don't think you better try. We know you are an expert in the martial arts and hand to hand combat but so are we. Neither of us one on one has ever been beaten by anyone male or female."

"I think you had better listen to them," a deep rasping voice said behind Judith. It was the D.A.D. Both women came to attention. "At ease soldiers. You see Judith these women are acting under my orders, so if you will excuse me, I've got work to do. Oh, by the way, if you need help with those, they will be glad to help you." Then he walked away from Judith and began to talk to one of the men just down the hall. She noticed the man talking to the D.A.D. was dressed in fatigues just as the women were. He also was African American with curly hair.

That was odd she thought. She could have sworn she'd seen him up front when she was first confronted with the twins. "All right well, if you women are going to help me with those boxes then let's go," Judith said with hands on her hips.

"Yes, ma'am," they said and began picking up two boxes at a time carrying them out of the truck. The way the women carried the boxes so effortlessly made it seem like the boxes were empty.

As Judith walked up front, she met the man wearing fatigues who had been talking to the D.A.D. He was coming up the steps into the truck. There was not another door to this vehicle, so there had to be two of them. Why did he have twins working for him? Probably just a coincidence she thought. When she got outside the women had put the boxes in two identical piles. Judith started to pick up one but found it too heavy to pick up with just one hand.

"Which truck are you going to ma'am?" one of the women asked her from behind.

Judith turned to the side. "The truck right behind this one."

The women then each took a set of boxes. Stooping down they grabbed the bottom box and picked the boxes up with one heave and stood waiting for Judith to point the way. Judith just stood there with her mouth open in total disbelief.

"If I didn't see it with my own eyes, I would not have believed it," she said as she walked down to the second truck. She ordered them to put the boxes down in front of the door and dismissed them. When she went inside the truck, she would be operating from she found her men had already arrived. "How did you guys know to come here?" she asked.

The men looked at each other and then one of them stood up. "The D.A.D. told us this was the one you would want. He said you would want to keep close tabs on him, so this would be the one you would pick."

"Oh, he did, did he? Well I'll tell you what." she said annoyed and losing her composure as well. "We'll just go down to the last truck and set up shop there."

The men looked at each other again. "He said you would suggest that so he told us to tell you those would be off-limits to all but his personnel."

Judith slammed her purse down on the chair next to her and yelled, "That tears it." She pushed one man out of her way and picked up the phone of the command module and started to dial her boss's number. "Up to now, I have put up with this crap but no more."

"First district headquarters Delaney here. What is your first line of code?" he asked.

"Little Red Riding hood was eaten by her grandmother," Judith responded. There was a slight pause.

"I knew you were going to call Judith and I have to tell you to take his orders or come back and get another assignment," her boss said.

Judith was stunned and struggled to calm herself as she sat down in the chair.

"As far as I am concerned, I put you on the job and it was yours, but this came from higher up, and there is nothing I can do about it."

"But you outrank this guy. Who is he, anyway?" Judith asked.

"Play ball with the guy. Give him what he wants, and you can keep playing. Besides he's after the same thing you and I are after," Delaney reminded Judith.

"I don't know about that," Judith said hesitating for a minute. "What's with all the people of color and the twins?"

"I think it's because he's Afro-American."

"What?" Judith said being visibly shocked. "He looks just as white as you or I. Then how did he get so much power?"

"It comes from high up," Delaney answered. "Hold on Judith." Delaney took her offline and put her on hold for a couple of minutes. When he came back, it was to end their conversation. "I've got to go, but before I go let me give you some advice all the windows have eyes." And then they were disconnected.

"Delaney, Delaney," Judith shouted into the phone, but it was too late. The only reason she could think he said (the windows have eyes) was that the phone was being monitored. When she thought on the situation, it did not surprise her after all. She got up from where she was seated and noticed the men were all staring at her. "Put together a report on all we have found out on this case so far. I'll look it over later."

Never Die On A Cold Night II
<u>REVELATIONS</u>

"When do you want it, Ma'am?" her assistant asked.

"Right now," she said. As she started to leave one of the men on the radio summoned her.

"It's Charley," he said.

"All right, I'll take it from back here. Somebody get me my stuff. Those boxes outside are mine. You may find some paperwork inside to use to work on the project." With that, she went to the office in the back of the trailer. Looking around the office, she saw there was a toilet and shower and a small bedroom which was all she needed. She picked up the phone.

"Hello, Judith."

"Hello, and to what do I owe this unexpected intrusion."

"How about a truce?"

"Ah, a truce, is it?"

"Yes. Listen Judith."

"I'm listening."

"I realize what you told me is right. I think we had better work together to find the murderer and to find David. The murderer of those two girls had to be the Red Pack."

"Why the change of heart?"

"I found something out about the D.A.D., he is not who he claims to be. It's possible—"

"Wait a minute, Charley, the walls have ears. I'm going to have to meet you somewhere. Call me on the two-way we used the first time. Use the first code, and we will talk more then."

By
J. P. Leonard

Charley hung up the phone. There was a click on the opposite end and then the lone sound of a dial tone. Someone was listening.

"Did she buy it?" a voice said from outside the booth Charley occupied.

Without looking out of the booth but staring strangely at the phone, Charley answered. "Hook line and sinker."

The man outside the booth wore the insignia of a major on his dress blue uniform which gave credibility to the many ribbons displayed over his front coat pocket. Although he must have been in his fifties, his appearance suggested he had stopped aging around the age of thirty-something. His strong and somehow boyish face gave him the appearance of a golden-haired angel.

Charley and the major walked back to where they had been sitting and sat down, Charley looked into the cold dark eyes of the man. "What are you going to do to her?"

"Kill her of course," the man said. The major was a slender but well-built man, and the uniform made him look even the more tough. The hash marks on his sleeve depicted a long term of service in the U.S. Navy.

"Do you think that's necessary?"

"The D.A.D. does, and that's all you need to know. We'll help you to get Detective Neal, but you must keep your part of the bargain. We need every bit of the information on all the murders of this kind of the cases you've been in on. Everything Detective Neal has worked on, as well as yourself. The D.A.D. will be very appreciative of all you can do."

"How do I know everything you have told me is true?" Charley asked the man.

Never Die On A Cold Night II
REVELATIONS

The man pulled a package from inside his coat and held it out for Charley to take. "This disk is highly classified. It is copy-proof and write-proof. You must turn the computer off and back on to activate the program. It will run, and then when it's finished, it will shut itself down. It will run on any operating system. I suggest you use it on a computer or reader you don't want."

"Why?" Charley asked as he picked up the package and looked over its contents.

"Because once it stops," the man said coolly. "It will explode inside of ten seconds.

Charley dropped the package like a hot potato and stood up so fast he knocked the chair back.

The man calmly sat back in his chair. "Don't worry Charley it's loaded but the safety's on," the man said as he continued to smile.

One of the waitresses came over to Charley and picked his chair up. Touching him on the arm, she asked? "Are you all right sir."

"He's all right Miss," the man said.

The waitress looked at the man and then at Charley with concern but got a call from another party excused herself and left.

"Sit down Charley," the man said as he chuckled to himself. "Do you know much about computers?"

Charley couldn't believe there was such a thing as an exploding disk, but then there were a lot of things he had trouble believing. Such as the FBI Wanting to kill one of their own, and this guy being used to do it. "Not very much," Charley said as he sat down.

The man looked down for a minute then lifted his face again to look at Charley. "The disk cannot go off by itself. When the computer is read in a certain section of the disk after it gives you the information it detonates then. It will happen as soon as any device reads the section but not before so don't worry about it." The major got up from the table and put on his cap. "Call me when you are ready Charley."

Charley watched the naval officer walk out of the restaurant. Even though he wanted to find David, he wasn't so sure if what he was doing was right. It was like there were two different people inside him. One wanted to get back together with his wife and renew his friendship with David but the other which he did not understand wanted a new life a new beginning with someone else. The second side seemed to be winning over at least it had been when Nicola was alive. How could David do that to him? How could David have killed the woman he loved. He took his fist and banged it hard on the table that sent the water glasses spilling all over the table.

The manager had been watching Charley from some ways off ever since he knocked the chair over. When he saw Charley hit the table, he decided to walk cautiously over to the table. "Can I help you with something sir?" he said.

Charley got up from the table abruptly and without saying anything to the man pushed him aside and stormed out the restaurant.

"What about your lunch?"

Charley kept on going without stopping. He was upset again, and it was nothing new. He got outside to his car where the two officers who were working as his bodyguards were sitting.

Never Die On A Cold Night II
<u>REVELATIONS</u>

"Charley, do you think it's wise to go off without us? What if something happened to you?" Officer Wilson asked.

"I refuse to take you guys with me every time I want to have a crap," Charley fumed. "If you guys want to continue to work, then we do it the way I want....Clear?"

"Yes, sir," Wilson said as he looked at the other officer.

"Good." Charley seemed to calm down. "Now let's find a computer store pronto."

"There's one about a block away from here" Officer Delfonso offered.

"All right then let's go, guys, we don't have all day," Charley snapped.

When they got to the store, Charley went in alone. Fifteen minutes later he came out of the store, and a man dressed in a white shirt and tie came out behind him. He stopped Charley saying, "I'm sorry sir nothing like this has ever happened before. Please accept our apology and this hundred-dollar gift certificate towards anything in the store. We will also pay for the program as soon as you let us know how much it was."

Charley shook the man's hand and got into the car.

"What was all that about?" Officer Delfonso asked.

"Just some incompetence," Charley said smiling. "We have got to get to the station guys. Make sure the report is done today." An hour later they were in the station. Charley had excused the other two officers and sat down to do the report.

By
J. P. Leonard

Sadie Phillips had just walked out of her house and was walking down the front steps when the door opened, and her son ran outside. Sadie turned and quickly reached down and grabbed the coatless child picking him up in her arms.

"Sorry Sadie he's getting to be too quick for me these days," her mother said through the door.

"How many times have I told you about coming outside without a coat?" Sadie scolded him.

"I wanna go with you, Mommy," the boy said with tears in his eyes.

"Jeffrey you know I would love to take you with me, but I can't," she said taking him back into the house.

"But Mommy—"

"I'll tell you what. If you settle down for Mommy, I'll bring you back a Superman comic book, okay?" Sadie looked into the boy's eyes as she held him close to her heart.

"You promise mommy?"

"I promise." Sadie put him into her mother's, arms.

"Mommy," Jeffrey called to her, "when is David coming back here?"

Sadie and her mother looked at each other.

"When he's not fighting crime, he'll be back," Sadie said as she endured the disapproving stare of her mother. The smile on her son's face gave her all the strength she needed. She walked over to her son while her mother held him and gently kissed him on his young lips. "Mommy will be back."

Never Die On A Cold Night II
REVELATIONS

"Okay, Mommy," the boy said smiling.

Sadie headed out into the cold afternoon air once again. This time Jeffrey did not follow her. She was so tired of the run around she was getting at the department she almost decided to quit, but she remembered what David had told her. He needed her on the inside to help him prove his innocence if necessary. She would stay on. She was determined to find out what was going on. She loved David and believed in him despite the overwhelming amount of evidence against him.

When she got to the station, everyone was staring at her. Even her so-called friends that she had known for years were treating her like a kid in trouble with her parents. She would have been preoccupied with her trouble all day if she had not overheard Charley Stilles talking to Judith about David. She had gone into the women's locker room which was directly next to the men's locker room and overheard them talking. Charley was talking to her over a two-way radio because every-time he ended a sentence he said over.

"Are you sure they have David, Charley? Over."

"My snitch is very reliable, over."

"I can't understand why you don't want to alert the squad. We might be able to catch him red-handed. Over"

"We could frighten Hanniz as well, Judith. Now I could have just done it alone, but you wanted us to work together, and I think we should so are you with me? Over."

At that moment, two women officers were coming her way. Laughing and talking and making fun of each other. The women were so loud she could not hear what Charley and Judith were saying.

"You couldn't handle him if he put it in your hands," one of the women said.

"Yeah, just like what you did last night," the other one cut in.

Sadie was leaving the locker room just as she saw Detective Stilles going back upstairs. She finally caught up with him as he got to his floor. "Detective Stilles," she called.

He turned around and looked at her. "Oh, hi Sadie," he said looking as if he wanted to get away from her. He kept walking. "What can I do for you?"

Sadie started to walk with him. "What kind of news do you have about David?" It looked to her like she had asked the wrong question by sudden reaction.

He looked around. "What do you mean?"

"What do I mean?" Sadie's voice raised a little. "I want to know what you have found out about David."

"Oh, you mean Detective Neal, don't you?" he asked. By that time the others in the office were starting to stare at them. "I don't have anything yet; we are still trying to find him."

"That's not what I heard," she said with her hands on her hips.

The captain had started to stare at them now. Charley was visibly getting nervous.

"What is it you have heard, Sadie?"

"I overheard you talking to the FBI agent," she said.

"Yes, is there more Sadie?"

"Why are you doing this?" she screamed.

Just then the captain came out of his office. "What's going on Sadie?"

"I don't know. I can't understand why he's withholding information."

"Is that what you're doing Charley?" the captain asked.

"I don't know what she's talking about, captain?" Charley said. "I was talking to Judith but just about the case. Nothing unusual."

"I think you better go on downstairs Sadie," the captain told her. "If we hear anything, we'll let you know."

By
J. P. Leonard

CHAPTER FIVE

"Back-Fired"

Later that night Charley was sitting in the place he had arranged to meet Judith. It was an old greasy spoon restaurant on the south-side. The place wasn't big enough to accommodate many sit-down dinners as such—there were only two tables in the place. It was rather more for people on the go who just wanted to get their meals and run. The food there was okay if you didn't mind an upset stomach from eating too much grease. Charley could eat just about anything if it weren't moving. He sat with both hands clutched around his Polish sausage with one end in his mouth when Judith walked in.

Judith looked at him with disgust. "You don't expect me to eat, here do you?"

Charley tried to gulp down as much as he could before he opened his mouth to speak. "Only if you want to."

Judith turned her head as to avoid looking at Charly's partially chewed mouthful. "I think I might have come at the wrong time," Judith said observing her surroundings. She had never been in such a place before, and she knew she wouldn't ever again. Between the smell of animals burned and the view of Charley eating, it was all she could do to keep from gagging.

Charley took about four sips from the paper cup of soda in his hand. He wiped the corner of his mouth with the lone napkin inside the bag of food after letting out a loud belch. Charley pointed to the chair opposite him at the table. "Sit down Judith."

"No. If you want to continue to eat your dinner, you had better let me wait for you outside."

"You too good for my black brother's place?" he asked.

"No, my stomach is just not strong enough that's all," she replied as she started to walk out of the door. "I'll see you outside."

Charley sat there eating his food mulling over in his mind whether-or-not he was making the right decision. It was a matter of national security at least that was what the FBI said. Besides he didn't like her.

Charley waited inside. His messenger was to meet him inside the restaurant, so he waited there. He knew Judith would stay put. She wanted this meeting just as much as he did. He was told earlier that day arrangements were being made to secure the release of David. He also was told the FBI knew David had been kidnapped but not by the Red Pack. And that no group like the Red Pack was ever employed by the FBI neither did the FBI believe they even existed. It was said that Judith was freelancing for another intelligence agency, maybe even Russia, and had fabricated the whole Idea about the Red Pack to cover a scheme to infiltrate the U.S. with terrorist so they could assassinate key FBI Officials. For the FBI to take her down now by exposing her might prove to be an embarrassment to the U.S. if she talked later. He was told a hit on her would be the only way to go. It was in the interest of national security.

Charles Wolf was a streetwise punk the FBI had used several times to bust certain people in the drug business. So, the Naval Officer decided to use Wolf as the messenger. He did not want to tell Charley personally where the assassination would take place, so Wolf was made the go-between. He worked out very well as an informant because he knew Chicago like the back of his hand. Nobody on the streets knew he was an informant for the FBI because he'd never had to testify. Everything he said was always right on the money. Wolf was in with the crime bosses in Chicago. They liked him and since he was such a great charmer of women most women liked him too. He was the most profitable pimp in Chicago which gave him the means to be one of the finest dressers in the Chicago area. Not too flashy but always elegant and stylish. He went everywhere always with two young women. It was his style. He was never busted for his association with prostitution. The FBI saw to it. They had convinced certain judges and administrators of the value of Charles Wolf continuing to run his business. The question of AIDS came up once, and certain officials of the bureau convinced them there was no risk of his girls being infected and carrying some-kind-of a disease because they always used protection and had physicals regularly. Besides, his clientele were not of the streets but men and women in high places. The girls were always young and beautiful not a one over twenty-five. Charles Wolf was smart. He never talked to his women about business outside of his own or to anyone else. He talked to no one. As far as Wolf was concerned, he had it made.

The door to the restaurant opened and a young, light-skinned African American man stepped in with a woman on each arm, one of his race and one white. He was sporting a long black cashmere coat with a black hat to match. Wolf always smiled;

how else could he show the diamond-studded gold tooth in his mustache lined mouth. When he came inside the building, he removed his hat to reveal a crop of long silky wavy hair tied back in a ponytail going down his back. Everything about him was neat, well placed and expensive. When he stood, he stood erect. When he moved, he moved with confidence. His clothes were specifically made to fit his muscular body. He was probably one of the most handsome men in the city of Chicago, and he knew it.

Not looking at Charley he walked up to the encased area to order three polish sausages to go. When he received his order, he took a napkin from his pocket crumbled it up and placed it in the ashtray on the counter. He then walked out of the building and got into a shiny new Cadillac with his ladies and drove off. Charley took his time and sipped the rest of his soda got up slowly put on his coat went over to the window ordered a polish sausage picked up the napkin and walked outside.

When Judith saw him, she blew her horn and he walked over to her. "Where is your snitch, Charley?"

"We've got to go meet him," he said as he got into the front seat of the car.

As they pulled off, Judith looked uncomfortable, but said nothing. Even when they pulled into the alley, she said nothing. But she drove cautiously. Inside the alley, they pulled in front of a black van, and the lights went off then on. Charley pulled out his gun and pointed it in Judith's direction. Judith looked at Charley but not with a surprised look, as he thought she would. Instead, she stared into his eyes and without a word knocked the gun out of his hand. It went flying into the back seat. She saw the van open from the back. She jumped out of the car just seconds before the car exploded hit by the rocket fired from the back of the van. Before the men could get to her, she disappeared into the night. Charley wasn't so lucky.

By
J. P. Leonard

By the time Judith had gotten back with the cavalry the black van was gone. Nothing much was left of the car she had been driving except for the motor and a busted chassis and some of the burned bits and pieces of Detective Charley Stilles. After the rest of the fire was put out captain Edwards came over to Judith and asked if she was okay.

She stood looking at the wreckage. "Yes, captain I'm fine."

"Is that supposed to be Charley in there or shall I say what's left of Charley in there?"

"Yes, sir." Charley tried to set me up. The van in the alley matched the description of the van involved with the disappearance of David Neal. She knew the Red Pack was involved. Apparently, they had wanted to kill Charley as well as herself, but her quick reflexes had saved her.

"What happened here, agent O'Brian?" the captain said. The D.A.D. walked up. He looked for a reaction from Judith but saw none.

"We were tipped off Hanniz was in the vicinity. We thought we had a chance to capture him."

"You what? Don't you know this is a group effort? You are not a one-woman army. Why if you were on my force, I'd..."

"Hold on, they thought they had Hanniz, the D.A.D said. Too many men might have frightened him off. Besides we have the jurisdiction in this matter. You are doing well to be included in this at all."

"We have the right to continue to uphold the law," the captain pointed out. "Tell me one thing, Judith." He walked over to where the car was and gazed at the passenger side door. "What side was Detective Stilles on?"

"He was on the passenger side, sir," she replied.

"Then tell me this?" He added as he walked around the car. "Why was the door to the passenger side still shut and the door to your side opened?"

"I got out before he did."

"You most certainly did. Don't you think that was strange? If you made it out, it would seem he would have as well."

The D.A.D. walked over to the captain and put his hand on his shoulder. "Look Dan do you think there was some criminal act committed by the agent?"

The captain looked at the hand of the D.A.D. as if to say it didn't belong there, but the D.A.D. didn't move it.

"Why don't we let the little lady do her job—all right?"

The captain walked away from him and walked over to Judith. "If I find out it was your fault this happened, I'm going to have you with my next bowl of beans."

A couple of days later, Sadie's mother was trying to cheer up a disappointed and confused Sadie. Sadie was standing at the sink washing the lunch dishes. They had not eaten dinner, and it was about four o'clock. Sadie's mother and son were going to a dinner given by a group of doctors for a retiring colleague of theirs. Sadie's father had been a doctor before he died and some of the doctors remembered him and wanted to do something for Sadie's mother in the remembrance of her husband. Sadie's mother came into the kitchen with a couple of boxes and sat them down on the kitchen table.

"Don't you think these are pretty, Sadie?" Sadie's mother asked. They were carnations.

Sadie looked back at her mother and then at the table. "The flowers? Yes, they are pretty mother." She turned back around and kept washing the dishes. When her mother walked over to her and put her arms around her, the tears started to flow. Sadie cried heavily on her mother's shoulders.

"That's it, dear, let it all out," she said turning Sadie to her and wrapping her arms around her just as she did when Sadie was a little girl.

"What's happening? They won't tell me anything. They are acting like nothing is going on, that David's not really kidnapped." Momentarily Jeffrey came into the kitchen. "What's the matter, mom? Why are you crying?" He searched his mother's face for an answer.

Sadie stopped crying and began to wipe her eyes. Her mother released her and sat down at the table. "Something got in my eye honey."

"Don't lie to the child like that," her mother scolded her. "You don't want him to do it, so you shouldn't."

Sadie went over to her son and bent down to face him. "Your grandmother is right I should not have lied."

"Then you were crying? Why were you crying?"

Sadie's mother came over and took him by the hand and brought him over to the table where she was sitting, and Sadie went back to the dishes.

The boy's grandmother looked into the concerned eyes of her grandson and began to talk to him. "Son, sometimes life does not treat us as kindly as we think it should. Right now, you have us, but it won't always be so."

"You mean eventually you will both die. I know."

"What I mean is you will find someone you will want to be with, instead of with us, before we go."

"Not so, Grandma I'll always want to be with you and Mom. I love you."

"I know you love us, but someone will come along that you will love as well in a different way, but you will love them just the same. "

"I may find someone else, but I won't leave you because I'll want to spend as much time as I can with you before you leave forever."

His grandmother just looked at him for a minute and smiled. "All right. If you say so, son."

"I think he's serious, Mother."

"Yes, I know he is. That's why I love him. Give me a hug, son." She grabbed him and hugged him tightly with tears in her eyes.

"All right now, young man you can take your bath now if you want to go with your grandma," Sadie urged him.

"You aren't going, Mom?"

"Why don't you come, Sadie? You haven't been out in a long time. It's not like you are going on a date," her mother said.

"C'mon, Mom. It will be great," Jeffrey said. "You work so much we hardly go anywhere. Please?" he said as he waited for an answer.

Sadie couldn't resist her handsome son. "All right, I'll go," she finally agreed with a smile. "You know you two sure are something."

"Yes!" her son shouted. He grabbed her from behind and hugged her waist. "Thank you, Mom," he said happily.

The dinner that evening was wonderful. The people who put the event together did a fantastic job, as far as Sadie was concerned. She had to admit she was enjoying herself until she met Jerry Wilson there.

"Hello, Sadie."

"Hi, Jerry."

"Sadie, don't you look good tonight."

She was wearing a white and green gown low cut in the front and back. Sadie could see something was troubling the very self-confident Dr. Jerry Wilson. "What's the matter?" she asked, genuinely concerned.

"Do I look so obvious?" Jerry asked her.

She just nodded.

"You know, I'm getting scared, Sadie. I have never seen anything like these cases we are getting."

Never Die On A Cold Night II
<u>REVELATIONS</u>

"Which cases are they?" Sadie said as she took his arm, pulling him over to the bar and sat down.

The bartender came over. "Can I get you something?"

Jerry looked in the direction of the bartender without really noticing him. Sadie gave him a nudge in the arm.

"Oh, I'm sorry yes give me a double bourbon." He turned to Sadie. "What will you have?"

"Nothing I have to drive. You're not driving, are you?" Sadie said looking at him carefully.

"No, I'm taking a cab. I will go back in a cab."

Sadie looked at the bartender. "I will have a Coke please."

"Coming right up."

Sadie turned her attention back to Jerry. "Now Jerry what is this all about?"

"It's these murders. The ones where animal saliva was found."

"Crazy people are always turning up everywhere, Jerry. Blowing up buildings killing people in restaurants. It's very sad to say, but this isn't anything new."

"I think it is. There is a different look to these shredding murders. I don't think the Red Pack is committing them. The Red Pack may shoot someone or even cut someone in pieces, but there are instruments involved. There are no instruments I know of can do the kind of damage we're seeing. The closest thing I have seen even similar is what a lion, might do to his prey. Except these animals don't care about being neat and this killer does. Which suggests a human, I don't know it's just weird."

By
J. P. Leonard

"What are you trying to tell me? The killer is maybe some man monster or something?"

"Of course, I don't want to believe it. Whatever this thing is it is very intelligent. Maybe it's a doctor or someone in the medical field who has gone crazy and believes he's some kind-of-an animal or something. This person or thing would have to have super-human strength to shred the bones, it just doesn't make sense."

"Did you take this to the police?"

"I took it to Charley, and he just about laughed me away. Now he's dead."

"He was blown up. No monster there."

"You're right. But I don't know, it just has to be something else."

"Have you taken this to anyone else?"

"No, Sadie no one else besides Charley and you. I tell you I don't trust anyone now, but you and David. You can't do anything, and David is not here."

"I understand what you mean. It seems like everyone is on drugs or something, letting a group as the Red Pack exist. It's like nobody cares."

"You're right. If there is a Red Pack."

"Jerry maybe we should try to do something ourselves."

"You shouldn't do anything. Whoever gets involved could be in grave danger."

Never Die On A Cold Night II
<u>REVELATIONS</u>

While they were talking, Sadie looked up and saw her mother coming over and bringing someone with her. The man she was pulling across the floor to her by the look of the forced smile on his face was trying desperately to be courteous to Sadie's mother. Her mother was always trying to fix her up.

"Hi, Doctor Wilson, it's very nice to see you again." Sadie's mother said only as a courtesy. She didn't want Sadie to be involved with a African American man; doctor or no.

"Hello, Mrs. Phillips, I was just leaving," he said as he was getting up.

Sadie wanted to say something but decided not to.

"As I said, so nice to see you again, Doctor Wilson. Say hello to Fanny for me," she said with a smile.

Doctor Wilson just looked at her as he walked away. Fanny was his mother's nickname given to her by her former employer Doctor Jack Phillips, Sadie's father. Jerry, as well as Sadie, knew why her father had called Jerry's mother the nick-name even though Sadie's mother never knew. Mrs. Phillips thought the name Fanny was Jerry's mother's given name not knowing her husband was having an affair with Jerry's mother and was referring to her anatomy.

"He's a touchy fellow, isn't he?" the golden-haired young man said.

"He's my friend," Sadie said, getting up from the stool and giving a disapproving look at her mother.

"Oh, I'm sorry. I didn't know," the young man said as he tried to leave. Sadie's mother held on to his arm. The young man didn't dare break her grip.

By
J. P. Leonard

"It's not the way you think my dear boy," her mother said with a smile. "He's a friend to the family."

This was starting to get embarrassing. Sadie looked at her mother and didn't say a word. She just up and left.

"Sadie, Sadie," her mother called to her, but she just kept on walking. Sadie walked across the ballroom floor of the host's mansion. It was a very large and beautiful place. She decided to get her coat and stand outside. A butler standing at the sliding glass doors leading to the terrace opened them up for her, and she went out on the terrace.

She truly missed David. Where was he? Was she ever going to see him again? The butler opened the glass sliding door again, and a man came through. Sadie turned around to see D.A.D. Fitzgerald. She wondered about him and why he was there. As far as she knew Judith had been in charge. The word around the precinct was he was taking over. Now he was here and moving towards her. He was a handsome man ruggedly handsome. He wasn't smiling, but he seemed somehow gentle as he moved and stood by her.

"Even mothers can be a little demanding, can't they?" he said in his deep, raspy voice. Although he didn't smile, she looked into his soft blue eyes and found comfort there. "I loved my mother too, God rest her soul, but sometimes she was pretty hard to take. I'm Thomas Fitzgerald at your service."

"I know," Sadie said with a smile. She liked him. "I'm Sadie Phillips at your service."

"Oh, I know as well. You are the clerk of the Third Precinct. A friend of David Neal a fine young man."

"Do you know him?" she asked eagerly to know.

"Yes, I have come to know him or at least I had," he said looking away.

"Why did you say it that way? Do you know something about what has happened to him?"

"Listen can you keep a secret?" he asked looking her seriously in the eye.

"Yes, I can, but it all depends on what it is."

"I promise it will not hurt you or anyone else if you don't tell anyone. It might hurt David if this information got into the wrong hands."

She was glad he was trusting her. It made her respect him as well as like him. "I won't betray your trust."

"Good." Pausing for a moment and looking away from her, he finally turned to her again and nodded. "Okay. There is a dangerous person inside your police department. An informant for the Red Pack."

''The terrorist group that's been terrorizing Chicago?"

"Yes. Somehow, the group has infiltrated your department but why and what they are planning we are not sure. I believe David is completely innocent of the charges brought against him, but because of the informant we can't take a chance and let him or her know."

"Are you saying they would kill him?"

"Yes, they might kill him. We do believe they have him."

Sadie was very happy someone believed in David beside herself. "So, what do we do now?"

"We have to wait for them to make the next move. This group is a very smart group of individuals, but every criminal makes a mistake sooner or later."

It was wonderful news. Finally, someone was as convinced of David's innocence as she was. D.A.D. Fitzgerald really seemed to care. In a way, this man reminded her of her father.

"Sadie remember, no one can know about this. I trust you. I know you won't tell anyone not even your mother."

While they were speaking the glass, doors opened again, and her mother and a doctor friend of the family Dr. Brown, stepped through.

"Oh, there you are, dear. Why are you out here in the cold?" her mother asked walking up to her. She then eyed the D.A.D. Turning to Doctor Brown she asked, "Who is this?"

"Let me introduce you. Mrs. Hazel Phillips this is D.A.D. Thomas Fitzgerald of the FBI"

The D.A.D. slowly took the hand of Mrs. Phillips and kissed it ever so gently and looking up into her eyes. "It is a very great pleasure to meet you, Mrs. Phillips. I was hoping to be introduced ."

"Where have you been hiding him, Edward?" she asked Dr. Brown.

Before Dr. Brown could speak, The D.A.D. asked. "Would you allow me to have this dance, Madame?" Everyone could see he was taken by Sadie's mother.

"I hope I am not too forward?"

"On the contrary my dear man. I love it when a man knows

what he wants goes after it."

"Mother, could I see you for a minute?" Sadie said. "Excuse us; we'll be right back." Sadie then took her mother by the arm and pulled her to the side. "Mother, do you realize how you are acting with this stranger?"

"What do you mean?" Her mother looked at her daughter curiously.

Sadie let her mother go and put her hands inside her coat pockets. "I mean you don't know this man and you look like a woman in love."

"What if I am attracted to him? I haven't been with anyone for years, ever since your father died," her mother said.

"That's just it, mother. It has been years don't you want to take this a little slower?"

"Little girl, if I go any slower than I already have, you'll be attending my funeral instead of my wedding."

"Mother!" Sadie said in disbelief. "You are not thinking of getting married again, are you?"

"Right now, we're talking about a dance but you should realize just because your father is dead doesn't mean I'm dead," her mother said shaking her head. Your father wouldn't have wanted me to pine away forever. You know, don't you?

"Yes, you are right mother, but it's just been so long I thought—"

"You thought I wouldn't want anybody after Jack. Well, for a long time I didn't, but I'm through pining. I want to love and be loved again. Can you understand? She smiled at Sadie. "Sure, you can. Now you must get my grandson I might have to leave without him. Anyway, you don't seem to want to have any fun so you can pine away for both of us.

Sadie's mother walked back over to the D.A.D., and they walked back inside to the dance floor. Once she was alone again, Sadie looked off into the distance again her thoughts returning to David. As she looked beyond the gardens, she thought she saw something in the shadows in the bushes at the back of the garden. She moved up closer to the four-foot wall surrounding the terrace and leaned against it, squinting her eyes. Whatever it was or whoever it was remained surrounded by darkness. She might have been only thirty feet away. Suddenly hearing the glass door open she turned around to find it was her son. When she turned back to see who or what it was watching her it was gone. She could have kicked herself.

"Mom everyone is leaving. When are we leaving?" Jeffrey asked. "Aren't you cold out here?"

"It's just thirty-six degrees, honey. Compared to what the temperature has been we are having a heat wave. But look who doesn't have their coat on. Let's get you inside before you catch pneumonia." She hustled him back inside. "I guess we can go now."

"Where's grandma?"

"We'll see her tomorrow, okay?" Sadie asked with a smile.

"Okay, mom."

CHAPTER SIX

Despair comes early this year

It was three o'clock in the afternoon of the sixth day of David's captivity. It was cold in Chicago, but where David was, it was hot. Why did they keep putting him in that room and why didn't they just kill him, he had no answer? There were two things he did know. He was tired of playing the game and he was very-very hungry.

He figured like the last time it had only been about two to three days he had been in the cell. This time the door to his cell stayed locked. This time, he was determined to wait for whoever would open the door. Maybe if he was fast enough, he might overpower them if he wasn't too weak. He could handle this. It was completely black inside his cell except for the light coming from under his door, his eyes had gotten used to the dark. David walked around the cell, sweeping his foot across the floor. He wanted to see if there was anything on the floor he could use. Nothing was there. Then he remembered something he learned in the service. Some navy captain had taught him a trick using his belt and a buckle, so he took the belt from his pants and waited. He sat on the cement bed and rested his back against the wall and waited. Patiently he waited, but sleep was starting to overtake him. He fought it until he could fight no more. Eyelids heavy weak from not eating he succumbed to the demands of his body.

He almost immediately was awakened by the hoot of an owl, once more into the same dream, he had been in many times before. This time he wasn't in the forest but was in a type of clearing. He was sitting with his back against a tree with a belt in his hand. A woman's belt. The clothes he had on—he would never have worn such clothes. While he was pondering on those things, he heard someone walking up to him. Hurriedly, he turned to see who it was. It was a young woman. A naked young woman clad only in a bath towel she used to dry her short brown hair.

"Why are you looking at me like that, John Woods?"

She called him John Woods. Then he remembered the last dream he had. When he had looked in the mirror, he had seen someone else. Her accent was strange. It sounded German.

"If it weren't for the fact we have been married for six years—six happy years, I might add—I would think you were seeing me for the first time," the young woman said as she sat down on a blanket next to him. She hadn't bothered to cover herself very well—because one of her breasts, her back, and most of her legs and thighs were uncovered. The towel just lay between her legs while she used the other part of the towel to continue to dry her hair.

Who was this woman? It had to be a dream because he was in the cell. Or was he? Where was he? She said they were married, and she was very casual about her nakedness in his presence. Maybe they were trying to mess with his head.

"Honey, what's the matter?" she said as she let the towel drop to her waist. She leaned over and kissed him on the side of his face. "You haven't said a word since I got out of the lake? There is no one around, John, so stop being nervous and talk to me." She stood up and wrapped the towel around her. It was a long bath towel, so it covered her well. She was, a beautiful woman. She walked over to what appeared to be a picnic basket walked around it and opened the top. She started to take food out of it. Looking up and smiling she tossed an apple to him. He caught it in his hand and laid it on the ground. She stopped what she was doing and looked into his eyes. "What's wrong John? You're acting awfully strange. You act as if you don't know me."

"I don't know you," David responded.

She screamed as he started to get up. It was like she had just heard the voice of a specter. The look of terror replaced the look of love as she jumped up from the position she had on the grass, clutching the towel close to her body. "John your voice. What…how could you sound—"

"What is it?" David tried to ask as he went towards her. She just screamed again. "Who are you?" she asked. "You look just like John but who are you."

All of a sudden, she started to run in the direction of the woods. David felt the hairs on the back of his neck stand on end. Something was about to happen he knew it, so he ran after her. Somehow, he had to convince her she was all right with him. Maybe together they could figure out what was going on. But she kept running. She ran until she was in the woods. David didn't see her anymore as the forest completely engulfed her.

Then suddenly he had the feeling of not being alone. In the next second, he heard a familiar but ominous sound. It was the growl of an animal; a growl that sounded like the growl of a large bear. It came from directly in front of him, and then came the scream that tore right through his very soul. It sounded like the very life was being pounded and torn from the woman's body and it made him stop in his tracks. Terror gripped his mind. Should he go on to save her or should he get out of there? Then came another loud growl and the woman screamed the man's name. It seemed as if all the horror of what was happening to her was in the last terrifying scream.

"John!"

It was if he were being pulled by a strong magnetic force toward the scream but he knew there was nothing he could do. When he got there, all that was left of her was a mangled and bloody heap of torn flesh. Then he heard the growl again. This time it was directly behind him.

Before he could turn around, he was hit in the head from behind. It was like being hit by a sledgehammer, but just as quickly as it happened, he was awakened from the dream. David found himself still in his cell. Rising up from the cement bed, he clutched his head, his ears were still ringing from the blow. How could this be? It was a dream only a dream he tried to convince himself.

After a while, the ringing went away, but the memory of the dream did not. In every dream, he or someone he was impersonating was attacked by some monster. In the last one, though, someone else had been involved, the body had been shredded to pieces like the bodies in the cases, he and Charley had been working. Then a light came on in his head. Was he clairvoyant? Was this the reason for the dreams, and maybe the reason for the lady? Somehow, he felt better. For a while, he thought he was going crazy. Now he could turn his attention to his problem at hand. He was hungry. The thought of a rat feast began to be acceptable in his mind. David looked around for something he could use to kill his prey. Nothing but his shoes seemed to be available. He was about to untie them when he heard the metallic clicking sound of the metal lock.

David stopped what he was doing and quickly ran to the side of the door, positioning himself to open it as quickly as he could. Maybe his captor had a weapon. He might be able to overpower him and take it. The probability was low that the person would be so vulnerable as to let him jump them.

After the last click he grabbed the doorknob and twisted and pushed with two quick motions, then swiftly opening the door. Not knowing what was there, he threw himself out of the door hoping to catch someone off guard, but there was nothing there. Getting up off the floor he went over to the door and examined it. He found there was a small electrical cable going down to a small device opening the lock apparently by a remote switch. So, this time the door was not opened manually even if it ever was; but at least it was opened. Now the question was, should he play the game as they obviously wanted him to, or should he sit still and wait for them to come to him? He was not feeling very patient. Maybe it would be his downfall, but he couldn't bring himself to wait.

Now as it had been the first time, he began to smell food. The smell of baked bread was in the air. The closer he got to the stairs the stronger the aroma got. As David went to the stairs for the third time, he thought about all that had transpired before. The man who spoke to him the last time he was there told him of a part of his life he would have preferred never to have heard. The mistake he had made stripped him of his dignity. To find out his government may have been responsible for the murdering of those people, and that it was no accident or mistake his captor was a military or government man and the head of the notorious Red Pack; this was the ultimate evil. How low had they sunk when for money's sake they would turn their backs on what was right? Apparently, his captor may have been in some-what of the same predicament as he was concerning the raid and massacre. Neither knew the reason. Did Hanniz think he really had seen something? What did he want with him? Or was it all a lie? David wondered. Well, he was sure he would find out sooner or later.

This time all the lights were on. When David got to the top of the stairs the door was already open. He was greeted by those same three lovely ladies from the time before. This time David was determined not to be duped.

Again, each young woman had on a short robe only going to mid-thigh. David remembered the bath he had been given by the women, and he wanted it again. This time it would be different. As he came up to the three women he greeted them, and they bowed to him as if they were Asian. They didn't look Asian not at all. "Where is Thomas?" David asked wondering if he was going to get a response.

"Thomas is at the table, sir. You come with us we give you a very hot bath," the one with the rose on her inner thigh said. She looked American, but she sounded Asian.

As he followed her the other two stayed behind. Every time he looked back at them, they would look down at the floor and giggle. "Why are they laughing?" David asked the one up front.

"They remember you from last time," she said with a smile.

"Was I that funny?"

"No. Hardly sir. They just not see so large genitalia on a white man before."

"Goody for them," he said, neither flattered nor amused.

Never Die On A Cold Night II
<u>REVELATIONS</u>

Looking around David saw everything was the same. From the table laden with much food to the waiters surrounding the table to the multicolored tent housing the bath, everything was the same. He followed the woman into the tent and she immediately started talking to the other two women in what sounded Chinese. They responded in the same language. The sweet-smelling bath was there overflowing with an abundance of frothy bubbles.

"I am sorry not to speak in your language, but they no speak English," the woman with the rose told David.

"It's all right, for what they are used for they don't have to speak at all."

They began to undress him. The old clothes were thrown to make a pile on the floor. The women were very delicate but amazingly strong. At times when he would lift his leg off the floor, one would pull the clothes off while the other would lend herself to be his leaning post. He would hold on to one while being disrobed by another. The two non-English speaking women had begun to smile and look at each other while they disrobed him. This time he didn't have to ask why. He fought hard not to be affected by their beauty or the fact their robes had already started to fall away from their bodies. They could see David was becoming aroused. The woman with the rose kept to her job. She did it with an almost clinical detachment. If she was moved as the others, she did not show it. She continued to test the water for his bath. When they had completely undressed him, they went and stood by the one with the rose and together they let their robes drop to their feet. Then they surrounded him and gently pulled him into the water.

There was a pitcher of water on the outside of the large square bath-pool, but David was leery of drinking any of it until one of the women picked it up and poured a drink. She then offered it to him while the others proceeded to wash his body. She saw his reluctance, so she put the glass to her lips and drank it all down. Then she poured another glass in front of him and sat it down on the edge of the tub. It must have been cold and good because he could see the ice on the inside and the frost on the outside of the clear glass. David watched her observing what might possibly happen; nothing did. So, he took the glass in his now trembling hands and drank it down. The water going down his throat felt almost as good as their hands soaping and cleaning his body.

Then they started to get out of the tub. All except the tattooed woman she waited until David got out. The other two, now wrapped in fresh bathrobes helped him out of the tub. They motioned him to a table with a white linen covering. They helped him to lay on the table, and they began to dry him off. The material on the table must have had some absorbent qualities because even though he was wet, it was dry. There was another table on the other side of the table with all manner of sweet-smelling ointments and oils. They wanted David to smell them before they put them on him, but he motioned he didn't care. He figured he might as well enjoy himself, at least until after he had eaten, and his strength had come back. So, he let them proceed with the rub-down.

When it was over the tattooed woman went away and came back with some white linen clothes. They helped him to put those on, and they gave him some wooden sandals cushioned on the inside.

"You ought to market these," he told them.

The other two women only giggled not knowing what he said.

"Now you ready to go," the tattooed woman said as they bowed.

It was apparent they wanted him to go. As they stood waiting, he heard a voice on the speaker beside him the voice he had heard before.

"Please, Detective Neal come and join me for dinner."

The tattooed woman opened the curtained doorway and motioned him with her hand in the direction of the great table in the great hall. What would happen this time?

"Where are you?" David asked his captor. He wasn't at the table. David saw only the waiters surrounded it and the delicious-looking food that was on it.

"Please sit down, detective. No harm will come to you for now. You can eat the food. It is not poisoned. Or you can just sit there; it is your choice," the voice said.

"How do I know the food is not poisoned?" David asked him. "You are not here to eat anything."

One of the waiters the holding a tray of plates went over to him and gave him a knife. "Please Sir," he said with an Asian accent, "take off whatever you wish to eat and put it on this plate, and I will eat it."

There's no way he was going to stand there with a knife in his hands and not try to escape, but he wanted them at ease. David casually took in his surroundings and did not see one weapon except what he had in his hand. No matter how small the advantage was, still he must try to escape. Logic told him there was no way they would put a knife in his hands if they didn't have him covered. Logic also told him if they had wanted to, they could have killed him already so he must be of some value to these people.

David went to what seemed to be a turkey with dressing and took a slice of turkey and put it on the man's plate. He looked at the man's face and saw he wasn't nervous at all. As a matter of fact, he was smiling all the time. So, he went over to the peas. As the man followed him around the table, David put items on the plate. When he had worked out the plan in his mind and saw he might have some advantage he grabbed the man and put the knife directly to his jugular. "All right everyone, unless you want this man dead, you'd better show me a way out of here." No one said a word. They didn't even move. David heard a rifle shot and he felt the breeze of the bullet blow past his ear, and the man's head jerked forward and exploded. David let go of what was left of the man, and the body slumped to the floor. Two Afro-American men dressed in army fatigues carrying automatic weapons motioned him back from the dead man, and they picked him up and took him away. Immediately, three women dressed in scrubs came over, and in minutes had cleaned up all the blood and food from the floor leaving David standing there with the knife in his hand. One of the other waiters came over and picked up a plate and another knife from the table and stood by him.

"Do you want to try again, or would you rather eat instead?" the voice asked.

David walked over and took the plate from the man got his food and sat down and ate.

After he had eaten sufficiently and drunk his fill, he sat back to see what was next. There was no reason for him to try to escape at-the-moment…maybe later. David noticed where the people entered the great room; it was a door opposite the door he had come in approximately two to three hundred feet from the table. He decided if he was going to escape that was going to be the way out. As he was looking at the door four men of color dressed in busboy uniforms pushing large white carts came wheeling them towards the table. All of the waiters standing at the table helped the four busboys clear everything from the table and clean the table so clean no one would have known food had ever been there. After watching the men, David realized this Red

Never Die On A Cold Night II
<u>REVELATIONS</u>

Pack was a more highly organized, and trained group than he had ever imagined they were. They were also very loyal. David didn't know if he'd ever seen such loyalty. When the area was clean, the busboys and the waiters left him at the table, and the two guys in army fatigues came over pulling a television on a cart. They proceeded to plug the cord into an outlet on the floor.

"Sorry for the slight inconvenience," the voice said. "You'll have to turn it on yourself."

"I'm not in the mood for any entertainment right now," David told his captor.

"I understand, but you might want to see this, David. It concerns your fate."

Those words got David's attention. He got up and walked over and turned the set on. He sat in another chair not far from it.

"Just sit back and watch David."

By
J. P. Leonard

CHAPTER SEVEN

"Walk on the wild side and die."

In a home on the West side of Chicago, Diana Belcher was getting ready to leave for work. It was going to be her first day on the job a day she had worked hard to obtain. Not everyone could earn such a high honor as being one of the finest on the Chicago Police Force. It was a great job and a great day to do it. Diana's mother Evonne was in the kitchen sitting at the table watching one of her favorite soap operas while nursing a glass of beer. Later she would be totally out of it, and the next Morning she'd have a hangover.

"I don't see why you got to do this, anyway," Evonne said to Diana as she came into the kitchen. Diana still needed to press her uniform her brand new officer's uniform fitted her small but beautiful figure so well. She had tried it on as soon as she had brought it home. She had looked in the mirror after she had put the whole ensemble on including the hat. The uniform looked great, and she looked great in it. First, she stood straight in front of the mirror. Then, from one side to the other, she inspected herself. She had never had very big breast's, and after the martial arts training, they had gotten a little smaller. However, her small waist gave way to a nice, round, firm bottom and her beautiful face more than made up for her small breasts. Getting the ironing board from the side of the refrigerator used to be a chore for her, until she had started working out with free weights. Now she could pull the heavy wooden ironing board from its confines with one hand.

Her mother looked her up and down and shook her head. "You look like a boy now, Diana. I thought you looked better the other way," she said in a disapproving tone.

"I get a lot of compliments from men, Ma, and it's their opinion that counts. Besides I'm twenty-six years old, but I still look like *I'm eighteen*." On that last part Diana had stammered. Stammering—she still hated that nuisance of an affliction. Though she had gotten used to it since she'd had it since childhood it seemed she would always have to be afflicted with it. Most people she met seemed to think because she stuttered, she was deficient in her thinking as well until they got to know her. She didn't think about it much around her close friends. It only came up if they were upset with her. Then even her close friend's words tended not to be so kind in the heat of the moment.

The only person who never thought of her speech as a deficiency was her old boyfriend Henry. She had met him at the tender age of sixteen while he was in the Navy. Right away she had liked him, and she knew he had liked her. He was not from her city, and it satisfied her because the guys around her at the time were always trying to go to bed with her. But she had remained a virgin—until she met Henry.

Henry was the kind of guy who was hard on the outside but sensitive on the inside. She knew he didn't seem that way to other people but then no one knew him as she did. When she'd first met Henry, she found out her girlfriend's boyfriend had told

By
J. P. Leonard

him a lie and said she was going to get him drunk and screw him to death. She realized something was wrong when he kept trying to get her into all kinds of compromising positions. It would have gotten out of hand if she hadn't spoken up. She'd told him "Henry I'm not like you think I am."

Then he stopped what he was trying to do and looked at her. He told her he was sorry with such sincerity it almost made her cry. It hurt him that he believed her girlfriend's boyfriend without really getting to know her. That was the moment she fell in love with him and he with her. However, their love had been destined to fail. They would go to the park holding hands and walking her dog, Ginger, almost every day. The first time she'd talked to him she'd noticed the smile he had on his face and the way he would listen intently to every word coming from her mouth. One day he told her it made him happy to hear her talk. At first, she thought he was kidding until she realized what he was doing. He would play with her sometimes in a way to get her mad at him because she was very headstrong and sure of herself—she never liked to be dominated. After he got her mad, he would sit back and listen to her argue with him because it made her stutter badly. He would sit and listen with so much interest and love that when she finished, he would hug her and kiss her and tell her he loved her bringing tears of joy to her eyes. After a while, she knew what he was doing, and it became sort of a game they would play together. They never seemed to tire of it.

"What are you daydreaming about now? I'll bet it's that boy again. It's been over ten years since you heard from him. He's probably married and happy to be away from such a stuttering fool," Evonne said. What Evonne didn't tell her, Henry had tried to find her when he came back to Chicago one summer and after he had written her a letter. From the letter, it would seem he was still in love with her even after all those years, but Evonne didn't like him. She didn't like anybody who threatened to take her girl away from her.

Never Die On A Cold Night II
<u>REVELATIONS</u>

"I know, Ma, I know he's probably married with kids now. I wonder does he think about me anymore? It's my fault we're not together. I didn't mean it to happen," she said tears welling up in her eyes. "My dope problem pushed him away and he probably never knew it."

What Diana had not known was that Henry did know. He'd wanted to help her, but he had problems of his own. After he had met her, being young not understanding the ways of life, he had gone AWOL a couple of times, then he had gone to jail for a couple of years. After getting out, his record prevented him from getting a good job, sometimes any job. So, he was without resources, and could never find a job in Chicago. He had tried to get her to come to his hometown and live with him, but she wouldn't go with him, especially after she got hooked on dope. After he had gotten himself together, he wrote her but unbeknownst to either of them her mother had gotten rid of the letter, and neither was the wiser. So, he went his way, and she was going hers. She had made a terrific comeback in her life; she was on the police force. That made up for all the problems and disappointments her life had been. She was now a cop. She dried her eyes, took her clothes to her room and became Officer Diana Belcher.

Later Diana got to the Third Precinct. She was given a quick tour and shown to her locker. She was even warned about Officer Delfonso to watch out for him. But she didn't worry about anything. Her confidence was high. She was third in her class in every aspect but one, shooting. She was first in that. She was an excellent marksman and quick on the draw. She figured once the men saw she was not just a piece of fluff they would give her the respect she deserved.

Captain Edwards needed more women on his team, so he had jumped at the chance to get her. He had told the duty sergeant that morning to have her report to his office when she got there.

By
J. P. Leonard

When she got up to the detective's floor, the place was buzzing. There were all kinds of plainclothes people there, and people in Army fatigues. She knocked on the door of the captain's office, but there was no response. The secretary outside his office had gone to the restroom, and when she came back, she saw Diana standing there.

"Hi, you must be Diana," the secretary asked.

"Hi. Yes, I am." Diana came over to shake the secretary's hand.

"My name is Trudie," she said. "How did you pull this precinct? Haven't you heard about all the things happening here?"

"I believe I have, Trudie. Which is why I elected to come here; I thought I might be able to do some good."

"Well, if you can you are a better man than what's already here. Please don't take this wrong. It's just people around here don't know what's going on and the murderer seems to know it."

"Well, maybe the murderer will take a woman like me for granted. Men tend to make that mistake."

"What if the murderer is a woman Diana?"

"Well, they are human, too, aren't they? By the way who are all these people running around up here?"

"FBI, C.I.A., Bomb Squad, S.W.A.T. team, you name it they all seem to be here. It doesn't seem to do any good. Whoever it is just keeps on killing." Trudie went back to her desk and sat down. "I read your file, and it's pretty impressive. Oh, don't worry everyone's files go through me. I'm the one to make sure your name is on the payroll. Oh, you might as well have a seat.

captain Edwards went to the funeral of Charley Stilles. He was supposed to be back so relax. Charley was the latest of our casualties here at the Third. Well, anyway, good luck Officer Belcher."

About fifteen minutes later Captain Edwards walked in and was immediately rushed by about fifteen people. When he was finished talking to one another would come. It went like that for about a half hour. It was a while before he could even get to his office. Diana stood up as soon as he got to the door.

"Sir my name is Diana Belcher," she said proudly.

But the Captain didn't even look at her. He just went into the office and shut the door. Diana looked over at Trudie and Trudie just shrugged. Diana was about to knock on the door when it opened. The captain was standing there.

"You want to come in?" he said as he walked away. He had a folder in his hands. "Shut the door, Officer Belcher."

Diana shut the door and went over to a chair. She was about to sit in it until she saw him watching her. She decided to stand.

"I see by your record at the academy you were in the top ten of your class. How is that Diana, did you cheat? Or did you go to bed with your instructor?"

Diana was shocked. Her first instinct was to bolt and run right out of the office, but she thought this must be some kind of test, so she stayed to see what would happen.

"Are you going to answer me or are you going to just stand there?"

"No sir, I mean I mean yes, I will answer you," she stammered.

"That's all-right Officer Belcher. Sit down."

Diana was glad to sit—at least she would have the support of the chair to keep from falling in case her knees started to buckle. She was certainly intimidated by him.

"I have your whole record in my hands," he said as he got up and started around the desk. "Frankly I don't see how you made it to the academy, let alone through it." Then he looked at her and sat on the edge of the desk in front of her so close to her his pants leg brushed against hers, and she moved her leg a bit. With a look of disgust, he said: "You were a drug addict!"

She started to say something, but he didn't give her a chance.

"I don't want an explanation, Diana. I don't want to hear anything at all out of you for the next sixty days. I don't want to know if someone has spoken to you in an unfavorable or unprofessional manner or tried to make advances to you or the job is too hard for you. Absolutely no drugs or you are out on your ear. Do I make myself clear?"

"Yes, sir everything is clear to me, sir."

"Now," the captain said as he walked back to his chair. "Until I place you with someone, I want you to work at a desk and help Trudie. Any questions?"

She started to protest, but she decided to wait. "No sir I won't let you down sir?"

"Alright, then Diana you're dismissed. Close the door on the way out."

When Diana got outside the office, she almost broke down, but she didn't.

Never Die On A Cold Night II
<u>REVELATIONS</u>

"How did it go?" Trudie asked.

"Fine," Diana stammered.

"Everybody knows he's a jerk. Nobody likes him, and on top of that, he's very strange. I never see him with a woman or anybody else even though he's supposed to be married. He is always alone."

"A lone wolf?"

"Yeah, something like that."

Diana walked over to Trudie's desk and sat down. "I'm supposed to work with you until he finds somebody for me to ride with," Diana explained.

"Great. Then my first order of business is for us to have a hamburger and a coke at the hamburger joint near here."

"You're the boss," Diana said and the two of them went out to get themselves a burger.

CHAPTER EIGHT

"Let's go down memory lane."

Hanniz had successfully captured Detective David Neal and had him brought back to that dungeon of a prison again. But this time instead of sending him back to his home, they had clothed him feed him and sat him before a seemingly tv screen to watch what...he didn't know. Coming to terms with his captives, David sat down on the chair again and picked up a glass poured some juice from a pitcher on the table and proceeded to drink. He sat looking at the monitor they'd sat before him. Finally, the video came on and showed the news from one of the main channels for the Chicago area.

"Our top story is of an utter bizarre nature," the anchor-woman said.

"Yes, tonight we are going to come to you with a live report from our man on the scene Jim Patterson and a taped interview with the police captain of the Third Precinct. Here we have Jim Patterson, our man on the street. "Jim, tell us what you found," the co-anchor Chuck Waverly, said.

Never Die On A Cold Night II
REVELATIONS

"Thank you, Chuck. It's dark and cold tonight, especially in the city's police department. The murder suspect of Patricia Hill and Nicole Howard, Detective David Neal, is now wanted for the killing of his partner Charles Stilles."

"What!" David yelled. "What happened to Charley?"

"Keep listening, David."

The reporter continued, "As you know Chuck, we broke the story concerning the bombing of the car Charley Stilles was found. At the time we thought the group calling itself the Red Pack might have been responsible, but we've found out not long ago by a letter sent to the police as well as to our station Detective David Neal may have been responsible for the murder of his partner Detective Charley Stilles. In the letter and I have it right here. It says: 'The United States must realize they are no longer the power they have claimed to be. We are representing all the countries that have been stepped on by this so-called Democratic Government, who are the oppressors of the common people. We have declared war on you this day. To let you know we mean business and are not afraid of you. We claim responsibility for the killing of my partner Charley Stilles. At random we will systematically kill your officials here in Chicago until you realize you can no longer be the police for the world.' It is signed 'David Neal, President of The People's Revolutionaries for Peace.'

"So, there you have it, Chuck."

"Did you talk to any of the officials concerning this letter? What are they saying about it? Do they believe it?"

"Well, Chuck this is the interview we tried to have with captain Edwards of the Third Precinct." Then the scene on the monitor went to the front of the building for the Third Precinct. There, the reporter Jim Patterson questioned Captain Edwards as he went into the building. "Captain Edwards we received a letter supposedly from your own Detective David Neal claiming responsibility for the killing of his partner Charles Stilles. Is it true you also received such a letter?

"Yes, we did receive such a letter."

"Do you believe it was in fact your own Detective David Neal?"

"No comment." The captain started to move away.

"Sir," the reporter said as he started to follow him, "is this letter in any way true?"

"No comment," the captain said as he moved inside the building.

The reporter stopped at the door and turned around to the camera. "As you can see the captain had no comment concerning the letter given to the police." Then the scene returned to the TV station setting. "Chuck, that's all we have at this time. As we receive more, we will provide updates."

"Thank you, Jim, this is a very interesting development."

"Thank you, Chuck."

Then the tape stopped.

"So, you expect me to believe that?" David asked smugly.

"Believe your own eyes, David. Your partner is dead, and they believe you killed him."

"Why are you doing this to me?"

"David, we want you to join us in our endeavors."

Never Die On A Cold Night II
REVELATIONS

"Why are you trying to recruit me?"

"I am not going to underestimate your intelligence. I know you are looking for a way out here. You don't know who we are or who I am. However, be assured you will. I will tell you this, there is a secret locked in your head, and I want to know what it is. You may be unaware of the secret David—and if you are unaware of this secret, I'm sure you will want to know what it is. It has to do with the present government you call your own. They've duped me, and they've duped you. That is why we want you to join us. We are truly the only friends you have."

"Well, if you are my friends," David said. "I would hate to see who my enemies are. Why did you kill Charley?"

"It was an accident," the voice said. "Charley was working for us. We wanted Judith O'Brian, but she was too smart for him. She is a double agent, and nobody likes a double agent."

"You've got to know I am never going to work for you," David said defiantly.

"Yes, we know how you feel at this point, but we are going to continue to pursue you."

Immediately four armed guards came and handcuffed David to the chair he was sitting in and stood back. A short bald man in a white coat accompanied by a nurse carrying a tray walked up to him. The nurse put the tray down on the table and picked up a syringe. She took the plastic covering from the tip and laid it back on the tray. She then turned on a small butane burner and lit it.

"What are you planning to do now?" David asked watching the nurse.

"We are going to turn you into a drug addict David," the voice said.

"Why what good will that do you? What good will I be to you as a drug addict?" David said, as he started to struggle against the restraints.

"You need to be convinced David, and this will help you to be. This is the last of our conversation for now…until we meet again. Have a happy journey."

David looked at the doctor and then the woman. "You don't want to do this. I'm a cop. Why are you listening to that maniac?"

The woman looked at him smiling. It was a confident smile a defiant smile. "You don't know him as we know him," she said proudly.

The doctor cast a disapproving eye in her direction. "Shut up, nurse keep working.

David tried to work on the nurse. He needed some time. Though his situation seemed hopeless, he wasn't about to give up. Even with the dope in his veins, he wasn't about to give up. "That monster goes around killing people. How can you justify what he's done? look what he is having you to do to me. I'm a cop I'm telling you!" David told himself to keep control. He couldn't look weak in front of the enemy he'd just have to ride it out.

One of the men had a small receiver inserted in his ear David noticed. He put his hand up to his ear as if he needed to hear his instructions more clearly. He then walked over to the chair and motioned to one of the other guards to take his weapon. "Hold everything, doctor," the guard told the doctor as he handed his weapon to other the guard. He, too, had an Asian accent. "We've got to take him down to the operating room."

Never Die On A Cold Night II
<u>REVELATIONS</u>

"Under whose authority?" the doctor asked being reluctant to give up his patient.

"The master," the guard said as he began to uncuff David. Then another man appeared.

David viewed his surroundings carefully. The only way into the hall as far as he could see was through the two doors one opposite the other. He could eliminate the one he came through. The way out was the way everyone else came in.

The man stepped forward and introduced himself to David. "Hello David, my name is Doctor Albert Shacks. I am going to be with you for the next few days."

Doctor Shacks reminded David of a TV doctor. He had a black hair cut very neatly and a clean-shaven face. His eyes seemed kind and trustworthy, and he wore a gentle smile. His appearance suggested he was no more than forty-five. David was impressed by the man's attitude. He was cleanly dressed and very articulate, and he possessed a sure confidence in himself. David didn't care who he was or why he was there his only concern was escaping. The guard finally removed the restraints holding him to the chair and started to cuff his hands.

"Don't put those on him," Doctor Shacks told the guard.

"But I have my orders Doctor," the guard said as he continued to put David's hands together behind him. David had stood up by then. He watched the doctor's face as he spoke to the guard. A cold, hard stare had replaced the smile.

"Your orders have been changed. As far as the rest of your duties, you'd better check to see if you have any," the doctor said.

Immediately the guard let go of David's hands and stepped back. He could see this man had some authority here. It amused him. As amused as David was, he knew what he had to do. They had not killed him or tried to kill him. David took in his surroundings as the good doctor talked to the nurse and the other doctor there. David could see the first doctor was not happy about what was transpiring, and he was letting Dr. Shacks know it. They motioned for David to sit down again.

"How can you do this procedure on a human? The procedure has never been successful on any animals. Why chance it now?" the first doctor asked Doctor Shacks.

"I'll give you the same advice you gave nurse Bettman—be quiet." Doctor Shacks turned his back on the doctor, and the doctor abruptly walked away back across the hall to the door he had come through.

Doctor Shacks the guards and the nurse walked away from David huddling to converse among themselves. His opportunity had become apparent. Taking one more look around David sprang to his feet and had covered a third of the ground when the guard spotted him. David heard the doctor tell one of the guards, "You fool don't do it." David knew he must have wanted to shoot him. Nothing happened, so he sprinted through the door only to find a kitchen and no way out.

"What is this?" he said aloud. Desperately David tried to find some way out of his prison, but he couldn't find an exit. Not even a window. David saw a bunch of knives and grabbed one. He was determined not to endure any more. He was going to make them shoot him, or he was going to kill every last one of them including the good doctor. He waited inside the kitchen, right beside the door he had just entered. David waited and waited, but no one came through the door. Where were they? They had been right behind him. The guards should have come through the door by now. Cautiously, he peeped his head around the door to see what had happened to them and saw no one. Gripping the knife tightly in his hand he then stepped around into the entrance ready for a confrontation but none followed. It was if they had never been there. No one was in the room—no furniture, no TV, nothing at all except for the tent. As David walked back into the room, all he could hear was the sound of the sandals they'd given him slapping the floor and echoing through the great hall. He was alone.

He saw no door or openings except the doors across from each other. Either the people had somehow gone through the walls, or they were never there. He turned his attention to the multicolored tent and ran towards it. He heard the door to the kitchen slam. David stopped in his tracks and turned around. Why hadn't he searched for a trap door or something? As he ran back to the kitchen door all the lights in the hall began to go out. He was in total darkness. What now? Then he heard it. It was just like someone had suddenly opened several balloons at once letting the air escape. He didn't smell anything, but he noticed he was getting very drowsy. As his legs gave way from under him, and he slipped into unconsciousness one word came to his mind—gas.

After A Time

David didn't know how long he'd been out but when he opened his eyes a bright light flooded through his partially opened eyelids, and it hurt. He closed them again and tried to move his hands up to shield his eyes, but he couldn't. He decided to brave the pain, and he opened them again. As the pain slowly began to subside, he was also beginning to see more clearly the people surrounding him. Surgical caps covered their heads. Their mouths were covered by masks, only their eyes were visible from his vantage point. It was clear to him he was in some operating room. The round, very bright light over his head seemed to move down closer to him, then he heard the voice of Doctor Shacks.

"Hold the light for a minute," he said to someone. He pulled at David's eyelids to open them up further and shined what appeared to be a penlight in the first one, then the other. "David, can you hear me?"

David's mouth felt as if it was full of cotton, but he managed to pull out a hoarse "Yes."

"What I am about to do David, has never been done before."

"Then don't do it, Doc," he managed to say in response. "It might kill me."

"On the contrary," the doctor said in response. "In some ways, we are giving you a rebirth. We are going to give you a new face, one no one will recognize, and we are going to give you a clean slate as far as your memory goes. The part about the memory being taken is the part that has never being done—on humans of course."

"What happened to the animals?" David asked.

"They went mad," the doctor said.

"They went crazy you mean?"

"Yes, but don't worry. I believe in your case you will make it back," the doctor said confidently.

"Make it back from where?" David asked.

"The procedure is to take away your explicit memory concerning the events in your life without disturbing your procedural memory for things you have learned to do like speaking, walking, driving a car. That part is easy. But we intend to reverse the procedure, and that is the tricky part. If we succeed, it will be as if nothing ever happened and you will remember everything."

"What if it doesn't succeed?"

"Then there will appear to be multiple people or consciousnesses in your mind. As a result, you will go insane in a matter of days." He said it so matter-of-factly he sounded mechanical.

"Then, Doc, I don't think you ought to do it."

"I don't have a choice in the matter, David." The doctor looked up and nodded to someone directly behind David's head, and the individual went away. David struggled against the restraints holding him down, but it was no use. He could not move.

The individual behind David came back and positioned something like a breather over his mouth. He tried to move his head away from the object, but someone was holding his head.

"Count backward in bits," Dr. Shacks said. "No, I mean in numbers, going backward."

But before David could count all went dark.

Somewhere in another place a man before he opened his eyes, could smell the air; it was full of the scent of an ocean spray. In the background, he could hear seagulls calling to each other as they flew around him. When his eyes finally opened, he realized he didn't know where he was. Not only that, but he didn't know who he was.

He didn't see her at first, but as soon as he was able to lift himself up he noticed her looking at him. She was wearing a very revealing bathing suit. She was a beautiful woman with a very nice body. She had muscular thighs and a flat abdomen. Yes, she was a beautiful woman.

The man realized he was on a beach clad only in shorts and a flowered silk shirt. It must have been noon because the sun was straight up in the air. He looked up but had to shield his eyes from the rays of the sun. It was very hot so hot he couldn't think clearly.

"You're lucky you've been there since early this morning," the woman said.

"Why?" he asked her.

"The Sand! You would have been scorched by now," she added as she started to put some oil on her skin.

"What?"

"Are you a tourist here in Florida?" she asked him. "This must be your first time on the beach."

"You say this is Florida?"

"Say are you kidding or something? the woman ask. You're acting pretty strange; I mean there are a lot of strange guys around. People committing murders everywhere. Like those murders in Chicago. You know the ones the police don't know anything about, where the people have been mutilated. You know."

"No," he said, "I'm afraid I don't know."

"What do you mean?" she said looking a little frightened. "Everybody's heard of these murders. It's been on TV and in all the papers. You'd have to have been on another planet not to have heard."

"I'm sorry ma'am, but I don't remember. I don't remember anything, not even my name," he said. He tried to move to a different spot, the sand burnt him, then quickly jumped back to his last position on the sand.

"As idiotic and as ludicrous as that story you gave me sounds, I believe you," she said.

"You do?" he asked, stunned but relieved. "I don't think I would if I had heard it from someone else. How come you believe me?"

"It's your eyes. Yeah. Yeah, I would say it was your eyes. You have honest eyes."

The sand was getting very hot no matter where he turned. The woman next to him saw his dilemma.

"Here you can come over here if you promise not to try anything," she said sincerely looking at him.

He wanted relief from the sand, and no desire for her none whatsoever. Maybe it was because he had no memory. "Don't worry," he said as he got up and moved to her spot. He did feel comfortable around her, and the blanket felt good.

She handed him the oil she had in her hand and turned over on her stomach. "You might as well work for that side of the blanket you're lying on," she said, and he almost chuckled out loud. She almost made the feeling of desperation disappear by her little joke. She looked over at him. "So, why are you waiting? Do me."

"What?" he said.

By
J. P. Leonard

"Put the oil on my back, sheesh. Do I have to tell you everything?" the woman said smiling.

"Look, lady—"

"My name is Judy. Judy Leonard," she said.

"Judy, that name seems somehow familiar." When he responded that way, she looked at him with a very surprised look, as if she was disappointed.

"Did you remember something?" she asked looking at him intently. Then she noticed his expression of puzzlement. "I mean, I hope for your sake you do. What is it about my name because I have never seen you before? Is it someone you remember?"

"I don't know, I just don't know. Why can't I remember anything?"

"Are you sure? Is there anything you remember at all?"

He thought very hard, but all he could see by minds-eye were distant images and nothing else. "No nothing," he said disappointedly.

"Listen, look in your pocket. Maybe there is something there."

There was something there. "I have a wallet I think." He pulled the wallet out of his pocket and inventoried the contents. There were seven hundred dollars in cash, a calling card, one visa, and one master card and a credit card for Merchandise Mart. There was nothing with his picture on it.

The woman sat up and took one of the cards from him then looked up at him, smiling.

Never Die On A Cold Night II
<u>REVELATIONS</u>

"Your name is David Neal. That is, if this is your wallet."

"Do you think I stole it from someone?" he asked concerned. "Do you think I have done something criminal? I don't know why I'm asking you?" Somehow, though he knew he hadn't stolen the wallet.

She looked at him long and hard, then handed him the credit card back and lay on her stomach. "No, I don't think you stole it. Now oil me."

David started to oil her back. She had very soft skin, and it was beautiful and evenly tanned. She looked almost Mediterranean. As his hands smoothed the oil down her back, he noticed her very round but firm bottom. David had the urge to touch her there.

"You might as well get the thighs, honey," she said.

David poured the oil first on one leg then the other.

"Oh, that feels good," she moaned. "You have wonderful hands. Maybe you're a masseur."

David looked for a wedding ring on her finger. There was none. It was in the middle of the day and seemed as though she was used to being at the beach at this time, so he doubted whether or not she had a job.

As if she was reading his thoughts, she turned on her side to face him. "I bet you're wondering about me?"

"Wondering about you?" he asked. "What do you mean?"

"Yes, you're wondering about me. If you must know, I am a working girl. A girl for the evening."

"You're taking a great chance, aren't you?" he said as he lay down beside her and looked up into the sky. "I could be a cop, you know."

"Are you?"

David was wondering why he said he might be a cop. Then something spoke to him, told him to sit up and look behind him away from the water.

"What's wrong?" Judy asked.

"Do you see her?" David asked. Judy had raised up on one elbow, to look. David had only turned his head for a moment to try to get Judy's attention, but when he turned back again, the woman was gone.

"Who are you talking about?" Judy asked.

"You didn't see her?"

"No, I didn't," Judy answered. "You know maybe we had better get you out of this sun. Don't you think? She had started to get up from the ground. Then she looked at him, still sitting there.

"Whoever it is they're gone. Sheesh, you guys are all the same. If you don't like me, I don't care. I don't care if you see someone you would rather be with than me. Besides, you just met me. If you don't want me around tell me and I will leave you alone." She sounded a little offended.

"That's just it. I just met you. You might know me but I sure as hell don't know you."

"Well, I trusted you David might as well trust me; if that is your name. Anyway, whether you do or don't, it's time for me to leave so get up. She reached into her bag and pulled out some sandals. "Here you're going to need these."

David took them from her and eyed her suspiciously. "How'd you know my size?"

"One size fits all, dummy. Now put the sandals on. I got a place not far from here. You're welcome to use my phone then you can go to a motel or something if you want."

"All right, I'll use your phone." David got up from the comfort of the blanket.

After she folded up the blanket, she put a shawl around her arms. "Don't do me any favors handsome," she said looking hurt again.

This woman had a way of getting to a guy, she was probably good at her profession, though he was thinking. She took the hat off and let her silky black hair fall to her small waist. She was maybe a little taller than five feet, and he figured she had to be in her thirties, but she could have easily passed for twenty-five or twenty-six. She did seem nice and she was his only known friend. "Can I use your phone…please?" David asked trying to appease her.

She looked at David with her pretty head over to one side smiling, Then she suddenly grabbed David's arm. "All right come on."

She had a nice little place overlooking the ocean. Everything was light and breezy. They had walked up a long flight of stairs to a large deck serving as her patio. It was made of cedar, David could smell the cedar wood. It was strange being able to remember smells and not know where he smelled them. They were standing in a chrome and white living room with white furniture. Even the floor was white marble. David's thoughts brought a look of despair on his face, and she saw it.

"Cheer up, David," she said. "You could be dead, you know."

"Maybe I would be better off." he grabbed her arm tightly and looked into her eyes. "Judy what if I am a murderer or something? What if something is wrong with me?"

"David!" She looked startled. "You're hurting me!"

David let her go and sat down on the white sofa. He could not get rid of all the images going through his head. Sudden feelings of anxiety and desperation overwhelmed him. It was like he knew he had to do something, but he did not know what it was.

"Look," she said. "I have a doctor friend. Why don't you spend the night here, and I'll get my friend to come over and talk with you?"

"He makes house-calls, huh?" David said trying to joke.

"Very funny," she said. "This doctor will make house-calls, and this one's on me. Just do me a favor."

"What's that?"

"Don't call her him."

"I'm sorry Judy I just took it for granted you are—well you know."

"David why don't you just relax. Get yourself something at the bar while I get changed." She walked away into another part of the house and left him to think.

David walked over to the bar. A bottle of J&B was already on the bar and next to it were some glasses and a day's paper. He

Never Die On A Cold Night II
REVELATIONS

saw the headline of one of the stories on the part of the paper that
was visible to him. The headline read: MURDERER OF
MUTILATED GIRLS DAVID NEAL...And the top portion of a
man's face and hair were visible. Struck with fear he did not
want to pick the paper up from the bar to take a good look at it.

"Pour me a drink, David. J&B on the rocks."

David had to look at the rest of it. She must have just thrown
the paper up there. It still had the rubber band wrapped around it.
Something in his mind told him he was an honest man. He had to
tell Judy about the paper. She came out wearing white pants with
a thin white halter top barely covering her large nipples, and a
thin white blouse opened from top to bottom.

"Don't worry I'm not dressing this way to entice you. I don't
like wearing very much. But since you are here, I thought I
would be courteous.

"Judy, did you read the paper today?"

"No, I didn't. Why is there something in there concerning
you?" she said as she came around the bar where he was
standing. "Did you read it?"

"No. I was afraid to."

"Here let me see it," she said as she grabbed the paper still on
the bar and began to unravel it. Then she read it silently and put
it down on the bar. She didn't say anything she sort of backed
away a little.

"What did it say, Judy?"

"Nothing don't worry about it. I forgot something in my room,
I'll be right back."

After she left, David picked up the paper and read it. It said he was a murderer all right. It said he murdered several people, but it just did not fit. He could not have done those things.

Judy come back with her hand behind her back. When she was close enough, she pulled from behind her back a very large .45 and pointed it at him. "I am going to give you ten seconds to get out of here, and if you are not gone, I am going to shoot you."

"But, Judy, I—"

"Nine."

"I thought you trusted me."

"Eight."

"Please help me!"

"Seven, Six, five…"

"All right, I'll go."

"Four." The woman had changed into a different person. "Three." Before she could get to two, he was through the door and running down the steps. Judy went over to her telephone and calmly set the gun down on the bar. She dialed a number and waited for the party on the other end to answer and then she spoke in a plain voice. "The pigeon has flown the coop. He's all yours."

"Good," the party on the other end acknowledged. "I'll let him know."

CHAPTER NINE

"The Long road home."

The D.A.D and Mrs. Phillips were sitting in one of the most expensive restaurants in the city, gazing into each other's eyes.

"I am having the most wonderful time just sitting here talking to you, D.A.D Fitzgerald."

"Mrs. Phillips, I thought my current assignment would be another lengthy and dreary piece of duty until I met you."

A waiter gingerly walked over with a telephone and brought it to the D.A.D. He sat it down in front of him. "It's for you sir," the waiter said.

"Thank you," the D.A.D said. He put his hand over the receiver. "Excuse me, my dear." Putting the receiver to his ear, he began to speak to the party on the other end. "Yes—all right. You've all done well." The D.A.D paused for a few seconds and then hung up the phone.

"Is everything all right?"

The D.A.D's eyes softened as he looked at her. "Everything is just fine."

LATER THAT NIGHT

That night at eleven o'clock the D.A.D's truck sat outside of a warehouse on the west side of town. Several people were working very hard to get some new equipment installed, equipment supposing to enhance their security systems. They were having difficulties, and the whole system had to be shut down to get the new equipment online.

"Yes, Sir," one of the sergeants on duty responding to the man on the other end. "Yes, sir, yes, sir. I'll make sure sir. I'll call you as soon as we do, yes, sir. Good-bye, sir, and have a good evening. As the man got off the phone, he walked over to where the three army personnel were on the floor under one of the consoles. He stooped down to view their progress. "How long is this going to take? We can't see anything until we get back online."

One of the men had a screwdriver in his hand and was trying to attach some cable. "This cable is too small for the job. It is not going to handle the load of this transformer. If you want to get this hooked up, then you are going to have to send somebody somewhere to get some heavier cable."

"How long will the smaller cable work?" the sergeant asked.

Never Die On A Cold Night II
<u>REVELATIONS</u>

"This is speaker cable. Maybe five minutes before it fries."

The sergeant swore out loud. One of the women who had helped Judith move her boxes was sitting at one of the non-operating consoles.

"I'll go. I know of a place not too far from here that's open twenty-four hours a day. Besides, I need a cigarette," she said.

The sergeant looked at her for a minute. Then he looked at his watch. "All right go ahead. Do you have enough money? Do you know what he needs?"

"Yes, to both questions, sarge," she said as she started to put her coat on.

"Be careful out there."

"I'll be fine."

"Take the radio with you and the jeep," the sergeant told her.

"I'll take the radio, but the place isn't too far, so I'm going to walk."

"You know there's a killer out there?" the man under the console with the screwdriver in his hand said. "If I were you, I'd take the jeep."

The woman put her coat down and started to flex her muscles. "That's just it, Fowler, you're not me."

When they saw her flexing her muscles, they all started laughing at Fowler. She put her coat on and left the trailer.

It was quite cold, so cold she started to go back inside to get the keys to the jeep. "What the hell it's not far anyway," she said lighting up her cigarette. She started walking.

By
J. P. Leonard

It was very quiet going to the store. Nobody was on the streets not even cars. It was a surprisingly clear night, no clouds in the sky at all. The full moon illuminated the driveways and alley as she walked by. Phyllis was not afraid of anything. Neither was her twin sister, Patrice. Phyllis had seen combat in Nicaragua, so Chicago was a piece of cake. As she went past a large moving van, she thought she saw something out of the corner of her eye. She stopped and turned to see. There was nothing there, so she kept walking. Finally, she made it to the store.

A couple of shady characters were huddled together in the dark around the corner of the store watching her. She decided to have some fun. She walked over to the tough-looking guys. Both looked to be twice her size. They were both big and tall. She could tell one was a little overweight, but the other was moving around like he was freezing or high on something. She hated drugs and the people who took them. She hated, even more, the scum that waited and preyed on innocent victims. And these guys were certainly waiting for someone.

"What are you boy's waiting for?" she asked smiling.

The one guy spoke up, but the fat one was quiet and just looked at her with a cold stare. He's got the gun she thought. "We're waiting for you sugar."

"I don't want no trouble with you two punks do you hear me?" she said.

"Did you hear her Zimbo man?" he said as he looked over at his fat partner then back to her again. "Listen, babe, give us your money, and we might let you live."

"So, if I give you this money I got in my pocket, you'll leave me alone?" she asked as she reached into her pocket.

"Yeah, sure babe," the man said as he continued to move from side to side. "Just give us the money."

The fat man was more relaxed now that it seemed to be going okay. He'd had his hands inside his coat and now he took them out, leaning against the building with his arms crossed.

Phyllis quickly pulled out her pistol and before they could react, she aimed the pistol at the smaller man's leg and fired. He screamed and went down to the ground. She immediately put the gun in the face of the fat man, "Don't go for it or you'll die."

Tears started to well up in the fat man's eyes. "Don't shoot me. Please don't shoot me," he begged Phyllis.

"Give me that piece you got in your pocket," she commanded him.

"It's just a zip gun," he said pathetically.

"I don't care if it's a water gun give it to me, fat man but easy." Phyllis backed away from the man as he went into his pocket.

"Let it drop right on the ground easy," she said. The man complied still pleading with her. Where was his cool now? "All right, pick up your friend and take him to the hospital. Get out of here before I change my mind."

The man helped his friend up. The smaller man limped while the fat man helped him over to a car, got into it and drove off. As they left, they screamed obscenities at her, but when she pointed the gun at them, they sped off into the night burning rubber as they went.

"Wimps," she said, laughing as she went into the store. She finally found the item she came after and headed back to the trailer. As she got close to the empty trailers parked beside the loading dock, she saw something run behind one of the trailers.

"Well, you wimps are back for more, I guess." She walked back between the trailers. "This time I'm going to kick your behind."

As she walked back behind the trailer with her gun out, she was smiling. She thought she had them trapped, but when she got there, no one was there. She went all around the trailer but didn't see anything. She could have sworn she'd seen something. She looked up and down the street. She didn't see anything—no cars, no people, nothing. Her heart had started to pump a little faster. "Phyllis you're getting spooked," she laughed out loud and started back up to the street. She had just put her gun back into her pocket when it came from out in front of the trailer and stood perfectly still in front of her. For a second her heart seemed to stop. What was it? She had never in her life seen anything like it. It just stood motionless, right in front of her, just six feet away from her it stood looking at her as if it knew she knew all hope was lost. It looked ten feet tall with a head bigger than a lion's head. The mouth was larger than a dog's mouth, and it was partially opened and drooling. It was so close to her she could smell its foul breath.

It had long hair covering its body. The arms were long and as large as tree trunks. The legs were three times as large. She wondered if this was what she had seen earlier. It was very fast but so was she. She took one step back it took one step forward. It was toying with her. Phyllis looked into its huge, round, bloodshot eyes, and it almost seemed as if it was laughing at her. She had never been so terrified in her life. She was so, terrified she lost control of her bodily functions. But with every ounce of courage she had left, she tried to pull herself together, and in that moment, she reacted. She quickly reached into her pocket and pulled the gun out. She was able to get one shot off before a huge hairy paw knocked the gun out of her hand. With the other hand, it made a swipe at her with so much force and speed she hardly felt her flesh being split open and her ribs splintering, or her heart being shredded before she fell to the ground. For a few seconds, she could feel the horrifying pain of her flesh being torn away and her bones cracking with ever swipe of its hands. Then it leaned over her quickly and took a large bite out of her neck. The monster took three quick sniffs stood up and ran quickly into the trees surrounding the warehouse.

The murder scene was a total mess. Every department of the police force seemed to be represented. The FBI had stepped up its presence. The whole investigation had been stepped up. To Diana new on the force it looked like a circus. The photographers were tripping over the forensics team the sheriff's department deputies were tripping over the uniformed police officers everybody was getting in everybody else's way.

Diana was to oversee and handle crowd control but as far as she could see it was their own people who were trampling the scene. Except for the three people who lived in the area there was no one else out there. It was pathetic, she thought to herself. As Diana scanned the crowd of officials, she saw one lone man standing on the outside of the crowd surrounded by Afro-American army guards. She figured they might be National Guardsmen, but she couldn't see them very well. It was dark, and it was very cold being only a few weeks after the new year. Diana kept watching the man. The more she watched him, the more curious she became. All he did was stand there. She didn't think she had ever seen him go near the body, not even once. Who could have done this to this woman? The people she talked to had painted an awful picture in her mind concerning how the corpse looked. She hadn't seen it herself yet, but she wanted to. It was why she joined the police force for the adventure. When she was little while the other girls wanted to play with dolls, she wanted to play cops and robbers with her brother and his friends. They never let her play so when the boys were gone, and her brother had left off playing with his six-shooter she would play for hours by herself, and no one knew the wiser. She was in the top five because she wanted to be there, and she knew somehow, she would be a top officer and someday a detective for the Chicago police force.

"Officer Belcher," one of the officers called to her.

"Yeah," she answered.

"The captain wants you up at the scene. I'm to take your place here," the officer said.

"Have fun!" she said with a smile. This was it. Now it would get interesting. Diana hurried up to the scene. She noticed a reddish-blond woman very pretty in army fatigues taking notes standing alongside the captain. A couple of guys were squatting next to the body wearing white rubber gloves covered with blood. The body was also covered with blood. She looked at the face of the woman lying there, it was a look of sheer terror. She'd heard of people being frightened so badly their faces seemed to be frozen with fear but seeing it firsthand was even more shocking.

"Looks gruesome, doesn't it?" the captain asked her. He looked as if he was waiting for her to break down or throw up or something.

She looked him straight in the eye and lied instead. "I've seen worst."

The captain's eye twitched a couple of times in the corner, and the slight smirk he had on his face went away. "You probably have at that."

The woman standing next to the captain was staring at the him, then at Diana with a slight smile on her face. She winked at Diana and went back to writing in her notepad. It made Diana feel good that silent sisterhood acknowledgment.

"I know you are off duty at this time, but I'll give you tomorrow off. I need for you to accompany the ambulance down to the morgue you and Officer Wilson," the captain told her.

"Yes, sir," she replied. She looked at the ambulance. Right next to it was a uniformed Afro-American officer. He was kind of cute she thought to herself.

"Any questions Diana—"

"Phyllis!" someone was shouting out a name.

Diana and everyone else turned around to see where it was coming from.

"Phyllis-s-s-s!" She was shouting and crying now. It was a tall African American woman in green army fatigues thrashing around throwing her arms around and stomping the ground like a crazy person. One of the other guards was trying to hold on to her, but he was having a hard time. Another guard tried to help the other guard. Diana started to move over to the woman and tell the men holding her to let her go, but then the man that had been standing there with the guardsmen this white-haired guy went over to the woman, stood in front of her and said something. Immediately the hysterical woman started to calm down. The man walked away from her, and the two guards next to her let her go, and she calmly walked in Diana's direction. As the woman got closer, Diana noticed the woman was now completely calm. She also looked just like the woman on the ground.

As she came to the group, she looked Diana in the eye. "She's my sister."

"I'm sorry," Diana said sincerely.

By
J. P. Leonard

The woman walked past her and went to the dead woman on the ground. She knelt beside her dead sister's body and began weeping like a baby. "She's all I had with my brother gone and now she's gone," the woman said through streams of tears. She wept silently. She continued to weep for a while, and then looked at Diana and said, "bury her."

That seemed an odd thing to say to her Diana thought. She should have known there would be an autopsy. But then, this whole scene was weird. Some of the men in civilian clothes were walking all over the scene. Diana wondered what they were looking for. The men who had knelt by the body examining it had gotten up, to let the woman mourn over her dead sister. Now they put the body inside a body bag with the help of a few more men. The woman was so badly mangled, she couldn't tell how her physique had looked before she was murdered, but her sister was a large athletic woman, and since they appeared to be twins, she thought to herself there must have been more than one person to be able to kill her that way.

Another uniformed officer came up to the captain bringing yet another person, a man who looked to be about forty-five to fifty. "Captain this is Mr. Felts. He's the owner of Felt's Hardware down the street. He says a woman in army fatigues pointed a gun at some would be robbers and they drove off in a seventy-four caddie. We ran a check on a bullet we got from the hospital. It matched the bullets in the deceased gun. The hospital got it out of the leg of a man who claimed a woman dressed in army fatigues shot him. It fits the description of the deceased. We are holding him, and a second man who claimed to have seen the whole thing."

"Thank you for your cooperation, Mr. Felts, the captain said. Officer Decks, please take Mr. Felts to the detectives just pulling up behind us there. They're going to handle the investigation on our end," the Captain said, pointing behind them.

Never Die On A Cold Night II
REVELATIONS

One of the men in civilian clothes found something and shouted to the captain as the body was being placed inside the ambulance. "We found something. It may be the weapon," the man said as he approached the captain.

"Check the blood on it and check to see if it matches the deceased blood Jerry," the captain said to one of the men with the body.

"We can do it quicker," the reddish-blond woman said to the captain.

Diana wondered who the woman was as she walked over to Darren Wilson her partner for the night. "Who is the red head over there with the captain?"

"Special Agent Judith O'Brian. She oversaw the investigations with Charley Stilles and David Neal. Charley is dead and David—well, David is wanted for Charley's murder. Isn't that something?"

"So, you believe this David—he was a Detective, right?" Diana asked.

"Yeah right," he said, starting to get into the squad car. "I'll drive if you don't mind."

"No, it's your car. So, you believe David killed Charley?"

"No, I didn't say that."

"But I thought you said I was right?"

"You were right about the other thing."

"What other thing? Forget about it. Let's follow the ambulance."

By
J. P. Leonard

The next day at O'Hare David, confused and lost got into a cab. "Where do you want to go Mac?" the cab driver asked him.

"I don't know."

"Look bud I can turn the meter on, and we can sit here all day, as long as when the meter hits five dollars you pay up, or I can set the meter, and I take you where you want to go. The choice is yours."

"Take me to the Third Precinct of the police department."

"Sure, Mac. Everything all right?" the driver asked as he whipped the car into traffic. The driver radioed his destination to the dispatcher and continued in silence to take David to the station.

David somehow knew he had not done anything wrong and somehow; he would prove it. The only way he figured he could do it was with the help of friends if he had any. He didn't know how to get to them, so he figured he'd get them to come to him. He figured once they knew he was in jail they would come. And if by some chance he did commit the crimes then he needed to be off the streets so no one else would die even if it meant his own imprisonment and/or death.

The cab pulled up alongside the building housing the Third Precinct. The cab driver turned to him. "Seventeen dollars and twenty-five cents."

David hesitated.

"Something wrong, Sir?" the cab driver asked.

Never Die On A Cold Night II
<u>REVELATIONS</u>

David took the money from his wallet and gave it to the cabby. "No there is nothing wrong. But let me ask you, do you know me?"

"No," the cab driver said quickly. Too quickly for David. But he let it go.

David got out of the cab with his bag and looked up at the building as the cabdriver drove off.

"Well, it's time," David said out loud, as he started toward the steps of the building.

"David!" a female voice said behind him. "David!"

He had forgotten his name was David for the moment but turned to see who it was. It was a very beautiful woman, and she was smiling and running towards him. Although he didn't remember who she was somehow, he was comforted by her smile. Upon catching up to him, she immediately grabbed him with such force he had to hold on to the rail to keep himself from falling. She kissed him right there on the steps. He responded automatically to her, allowing the kiss to continue as he wondered who she was. The woman seemed to sense something was wrong

"David you have got to get out of here." She said it with such authority it made him question his own mind and the decision he had made.

"I'm here to turn myself in…Miss."

"Miss? David, you are innocent. Why are you being so formal?"

"How do you know I'm innocent? Do you know something?"

"Why are you acting so strange you are acting as though you don't know who I am."

"I'm…sorry I don't know who you are."

"What? What happened to you? Did you have an accident or something?" she asked feeling his arms as if that would tell her what the problem was.

"I think I have amnesia. I don't remember much of anything."

"We've got to get out of here David." She started to pull him away from the station, and he went reluctantly. She flagged a cab down, and they both got into it.

"Where to ma'am?" the driver asked.

"The Valiant Inn," she told the driver then turned her attention to David whispering to him. "We have got to get you a place to stay."

"I don't even know you," David said watching her with doubtful eyes. "I hope you know what you're doing."

She pulled out her wallet and showed David her Driver's License.

"I appreciate that—Sadie—Phillips." Slowly mouthing her name. "But that still doesn't jog anything." David put his head back against the seat.

"Don't worry, David, we will get this thing straightened out."

When they pulled into the inn, they were greeted by a baggage porter who opened the door for them. The handler carried the bag while David and Sadie followed. It had taken them a long time to get there, Sadie needed to protect David as much as she could. It was a quaint little place kind of up in the country about fifty miles from Chicago with lots of woods surrounding the place.

"What now?" David asked wondering why he trusted this woman. "If you were right about the police considering me a dangerous fugitive it might have been better if I had turned myself in."

"Welcome to the Valiant Inn can I be of service to you?" the handsome young desk clerk asked them.

"Yes, my husband and I would like a room for a few days," Sadie answered.

The desk clerk looked at Sadie then at David as if he were looking for David to say something. He reached down under the counter and pulled out a card and placed it on the counter top with a pencil. "Would you fill this out please?" David instinctively reached out for the card, but Sadie picked it up first.

"I can do it, honey."

The clerk looked at David and David just shrugged his shoulders and smiled. "Some wives just like to be in charge I guess." The clerk laughed.

"Are you guys laughing at me?" Sadie asked, pouting.

David grabbed Sadie by her shoulders and squeezed her to him "No, honey we were making a harmless observation. I love you I would never make you the brunt of a joke."

"No ma'am," the clerk smiled. "It would have been the farthest thing from our minds." The clerk handed Sadie the key to the room and motioned to the porter to pick up the bag.

As Sadie and David walked away from the front desk, David still had his arm around Sadie. All at once David stopped and took his arm from around Sadie, as he stared ahead of them his face starting to lose its color. Sadie looked around to see if anyone was looking and she grabbed his hand and gently tugged him towards the elevators. "What's wrong David? Why did you stop and pull away like that?"

"I thought I saw something," he said a strange look on his face.

As they got to the elevators, Sadie pushed the elevator button. "What did you see? You look white as a sheet."

The door to the elevator opened and the woman David had seen on the beach was now on the elevator. But she looked familiar somehow. He knew he'd seen her before the episode on the beach but couldn't remember where. "Who are you?" David asked as he started getting into the elevator.

Sadie followed him in and tugged at his arm. "David, who are you talking to?"

David looked at Sadie for a second then turned around to ask the woman again, but she was gone. David wildly turned back and forth, then tried to stop the door from closing.

Sadie stepped back from him. "David you're frightening me." The door shut before he had a chance to get to them; it made him start swearing out loud he banged his fist against the closed elevator doors. Sadie coward in the corner of the elevator. "David, what are you doing? Why are you getting so upset?"

"The woman," he said.

"What woman?"

"The woman I saw at the beach. I didn't tell you about her, but how?" David paced back and forth. Feelings he had before started overwhelming his thinking although he only remembered today as being the first time, he had those feelings; he wondered if he was losing his mind. The elevator stopped, and Sadie started to get out. There was an old couple who had started to get on but when they saw the expression Sadie had on her face and the wild look in David's eyes they decided not to get on. They walked away hurriedly.

David grabbed Sadie's arm. "Is this our stop."

"Let go of me," Sadie said.

David let her go immediately sensing her fear. "I'm sorry but did you see the woman in the elevator?" he asked, pleading.

"David you said something about seeing a woman before. Even the guys on the force were making fun of you about it. Maybe it was the same one, but I didn't see anything."

"You didn't see her?" David asked, holding the door open.

"No, I didn't, David. That's just it. I didn't see anyone. No one was in the elevator—it was empty except for us."

David backed up against the wall letting go of the door.

Sadie caught the door and went back inside the elevator. "This isn't our floor," she said. "I think if you get some rest, you'll feel better." Sadie pushed the button to their floor again and turned to look at David. She saw the helplessness in his eyes and tears started to well up in hers.

"Maybe I did kill those people."

Sadie went over and grabbed him and pressed her head to his chest and then looked up into his eyes. "No. Just because you thought you saw something doesn't make you a murderer. You need some rest until your memory comes back to you."

"You sound so convincing, maybe sleep is what I need. Maybe the answers will come tomorrow."

The elevator came to a stop and they made it to the room; the porter was already there. As they all entered the room Sadie watched David go over to the window by the bed. After Sadie tipped the porter the porter left then she walked over to David. "David, do you remember the dog you told me saved your life?"

"No, I don't," David said sitting on the bed.

"Well, I have the dog. Maybe the dog might remember you and somehow trigger your memory as well." She sat down next to him. "When we were in the lobby did you see the woman then?"

"No, I saw something else or rather I remembered something—I think."

"What was it, David?"

"It was you…ah I saw you."

"Well now you've got me curious," she said, smiling and looking into his eyes. "What did you see?"

He gazed into her eyes then. "I saw you and me making love—together somewhere."

"Oh!" she said. "You do remember. Did you also see where it was?"

"We were somewhere in a park or the country."

Never Die On A Cold Night II
REVELATIONS

Sadie's gaze turned skeptical. "Are you sure about that? Because if you are it couldn't have been us. We were never in a park. No, it must have been someone else you saw."

"No, it was definitely you, and it was in the summertime."

"We made love that's true, but we never made love in the summer. We didn't even get together until several weeks ago. Maybe it's just the way you remembered it. Maybe it was a dream or something."

"It seemed so real Sadie."

"I've got to get back David."

"Get back where? What do we do next?"

"Well, it's the job, remember."

"Yeah, that's right. If the police are watching, how are you going to make it back here without the police spotting you Sadie?"

"I don't know."

They sat there in the room contemplating what she should do. Since Sadie had to get back to the work they decided to enlist the help of someone else who was not being watched. Until they could figure out how to get together without Sadie being followed, or David was somehow exonerated, they could not see each other. Sadie decided to pay for the room on her credit card up to one week in advance. By that time, they would find another place for David to stay. She hurried down to pay the bill and left to get back to Chicago.

Back At The Station

Sadie called her mother. "Mother I need your help."

"What's the matter? Are you alright?"

"Yes, I'm fine. Are you going to be at home for a while?"

"Yes, for about three hours but then I'm going out for a while," she said cheerfully.

"Are you still dating Fitzgerald?"

"Yes, I am, dear, and I'm having a great time of it."

"Mother, you don't even know this man. You should take things a little slower."

"What did I tell you about that? Now what did you want?"

"All right mother I know it's your life, but I love you, and I just don't want to see you hurt."

"I am a grown woman Sadie. I took care of myself before you were born, I think I did a pretty good job of it. So, what do you want?"

"I need some information."

"What kind of information?"

"Let me come and get it."

"It's no trouble, Sadie just tell me."

"No, mother, please I would rather come and see you, okay"

"Well, all right I'll be here.

Sadie knew they could have been monitoring her calls and she didn't want to give out any information—of any kind. One of the officers from upstairs came down to Sadie's office and delivered a message to her, while seeming to be in a hurry.

"The captain wants to see you, Sadie.

"What's it about?"

"Detective Neal."

When Sadie got to the captain's office, she found D.A.D Fitzgerald, Judith O'Brian, and Captain Edwards waiting for her as she came through the door.

"Come on in Sadie," captain Edwards said politely. "Please have a seat." The captain pulled a chair over to where she was standing and held it until she sat down. Then he went over to his desk and sat on the front like a vulture perching waiting to catch his prey. Fitzgerald was silent. He sat in a position, where he could observe Sadie from a comfortable glance. She found she could also see him which is what they wanted her to do. Intimidation she thought. Judith was on Sadie's right looking as sexy as she always did. She didn't look the part of an FBI agent Sadie thought.

"Sadie, we have just got some new information concerning the murder yesterday of the FBI agent. We found evidence Detective David Neal was there and possibly had something to do with the murder. And maybe some of the other murders. David has been under a lot of stress. Maybe he's snapped and has started to copycat some of these other murders," the captain told her.

"How can you believe that? David wouldn't kill anybody."

"That's for the courts to decide," the captain replied. "All we want you to do is cooperate with us by letting us know when he contacts you. I don't have to tell you about what the consequences would be for harboring a fugitive."

"I understand, is that all?" Sadie asked defiantly.

"Sadie, I like David too," Judith trying to show empathy. "But we all have to do what's right."

"What's right?" Sadie said sarcastically. "Some people have no idea of what's right or wrong. One of the best Detectives you've got has gone missing abducted from right under your very noses, and you are so quick to find a scape-goat so that you could pin everything on him. The murderers would have to be the people who abducted him."

"All right, Sadie," the captain said as he left the desk and went to the door and opened it. "That's all I need for now. Just remember this is a federal case and it's a federal offense to harbor this fugitive."

Sadie was happy to get out of the office when she did. She didn't know how much more she could take. When she left the captain's office, she decided to leave for the day. She had a lot of work to do. She had to find David a safe place until they could figure out how to help him. She knew her mother and father had a cabin in the country but found out from her mother the cabin was sold to a doctor friend of her mother and father's. After she got the number of the doctor from her mother, she found a phone booth and got in touch with the doctor. When he found out Sadie was going to get married, he insisted on giving her the property as a wedding gift. He said it was the least he could do having been a friend to her father all those years before her father died. Later that day he gave her the keys. He said he would make all the arrangements with his lawyer to transfer the title to her as soon as he could.

Never Die On A Cold Night II
REVELATIONS

That night, Deputy Coroner Jerry Wilson was trying to piece together all the information he had gathered concerning the murders that had occurred earlier that year. He concluded someone had gotten into his report containing the saliva results and changed them. Everyone had been so busy at the lab working on everything that nobody remembered even getting the real results. Some of the files had been destroyed, and the computer system was down. No one could find what they had worked on, except for Doctor Wilson's doctored report. He knew they had not been able to find a match to any known animal. Now here it was when he looked at the file in his hands, it was saying the saliva came from a dog, the same dog that saved David Neal's life. However, the Doctor had made a copy of the original file and kept it at home in a safe place. He knew somehow it would prove to be a vital move to preserve the truth. He had tried informing the captain of his findings, but the captain did not want to hear his story, especially since the evidence found at the scene of the last murder had included David's fingerprints. The weapon they found was a type of human-made claw. It looked like a small hand-held rake, but they wouldn't let him examine it. While he was contemplating all the information, he heard the ringing of his telephone.

"Hello Doctor Wilson, this is Sadie Phillips," the voice said on the phone. It sounded like Sadie to Wilson but something seemed different about it.

"Hello, Sadie. How are you?"

"I'm fine," she said. "How are you?"

"I could be better Sadie," he admitted. "Everyone seems to have lost their mind. I don't understand, I just don't understand these people. Anyway, what can I do for you?"

"I heard the police have more evidence David killed those people."

"Yes, they think they do, but I can't talk about it," he said. "Sorry, Sadie."

"It's all right. But I have something which will prove David's innocence without a shadow of a doubt. Will you come and meet me?"

"Where?"

"There is a little cafe on the northwest side of town," she said and proceeded to give him directions on how to get there. "Also, I know you have files of the other murders. Please bring them with you when you come. Someone erased and stole all my files. I need to examine what you have and compare it with some information I saw which will be able to help us to prove David's innocence."

"All right, Sadie but if it was anybody else, there would be no way I could take files out of the office like that," he lied. "It's against police regulations. But don't worry I'll be there."

"Can you meet me there in one hour?"

"Sure. I'll get the reports together right now."

In the D.A.D's headquarters. A radioman was recording and listening to the conversation between the coroner and who they thought was Sadie Phillips. Taking the headset from his ear, he went back to the D.A.D's office and knocked on his door.

"Come in," Fitzgerald said as he kept his eyes closed,

meditating. He had been sitting in the middle of his floor on top of a linen cloth having a woven design of a pentagram in the middle of it.

"Sir, we just intercepted a phone conversation between a Doctor Wilson and Sadie Phillips."

The D.A.D. opened his eyes. "Well, what were they talking about?"

"Sadie asked the doctor to meet her at a cafe on the northwest side of town. She wanted to compare information with the doctor on the murders that could prove David Neal's innocence. We have the directions to the location."

Fitzgerald was quiet for a moment. Then he closed his eyes again. "Follow Sadie and get the information but don't kill her."

"Yes, sir," the radioman said as he went back to his console.

About ten minutes later a black sedan drove up to a black van parked half of a block from the house of Sadie Phillips. A man in army fatigues got out of the car and walked around to the side of the van. The van immediately opened, a woman in army fatigues got out, and the man went inside. The woman walked over to the car got into it and drove away. Inside the van, there were two other men with headsets on. One was monitoring a radio the other was watching a monitor. The viewer screen was large and split up into several sections. Each section viewed a section of Sadie Phillips' house. So everywhere Sadie went they could see her. One of the men took a case from a rack. In the case were a samurai sword and a black ninja uniform. There were two other cases one for each of the men in the van. Each man carefully put on their uniforms and covered all their heads faces and hands, until their whole bodies were covered. After the men had fully dressed, they all took their original positions. The man who had entered the van last just sat in the back and watched the other two.

"We must do it quickly," the man in the back said in Chinese. "We must not be seen by anyone, not even the girl. The doctor must die and all information the doctor and the girl have must be confiscated."

"How do we get the information from the girl without being seen?" the man watching the viewer asked.

"We will use darts."

"Something is wrong," the man watching the viewer screen said. "The woman got out of the shower and went to bed. She's not going anywhere."

"Call headquarters," the man in back ordered the radio man.

The D.A.D. was getting up from his position when there was a knock on his door.

"Come in."

The door opened, and the radioman appeared. "Sir the woman went to bed. Sadie Phillips went to bed."

Immediately the D.A.D. turned and shouted to the man. "Get them to the cafe we have been duped."

"Yes, Sir." The man quickly closed the door and radioed the van.

Never Die On A Cold Night II
<u>REVELATIONS</u>

The street leading to the café was covered with potholes. Deciding that this wasn't doing his car any good Doctor Wilson put the car in reverse and parked the car at a side street adjacent to the street of the cafe. He got out of his car with his briefcase and started to walk down to the cafe. The area was supposed to be both business and residential but because there were only a couple of houses and it was only twenty degrees that night no one was on the street. On both sides of the street were abandoned buildings and open lots. Jerry Wilson wondered why Sadie would pick such a place. The cafe didn't even appear to be open. The doctor stopped and put his case on the ground to button the top button of his overcoat. Just as he stooped down, he heard his name called from behind one of the abandoned buildings.

Jerry hesitated until he heard his name called again.

"Sadie," he said in a whisper. "Is that you?" He warily walked down a driveway partially covered with ice. He hadn't seen the big patch of ice, and as soon as his foot went down, he slipped, and his feet flew up in the air, and he landed hard on his back and hit his head.

Dazed, the doctor, tried to focus on what was standing before him. At first, it looked like a small tree or a bush until his eyes started to focus. Then he saw it. The existence of such a thing had invaded his dreams every night—the thing his mind had been telling him might exist. The possibility of a werewolf existing was so ludicrous he hadn't bothered to share his thoughts with anybody, but now here it was as big as life itself.

The large head was as big as a lion's head, the snout just a bit bigger than a dog's. He could see the fangs. It was huge, but it had so much hair he could not tell if it was male or female. As it stood there watching him with those red saucers for eyes, the

By
J. P. Leonard

Doctor's whole body trembled; whether from the cold or fear Jerry could not tell. He lost complete control of his bodily functions. The beast just stood there, then reached down with so much speed and quickness the monster had grabbed him by his leg and dragged him thirty feet down the driveway and behind a building before Jerry could scream. The monster took one huge slice downward and raked his long, sharp claws into Jerry's flesh cutting through clothes skin muscles bones and finally his heart. And with a yank, the still-beating heart of Jerry Wilson was pulled out of his chest into the cold Chicago night air into the waiting but salivating mouth of the werewolf.

C H A P T E R   T E N

"Friends are hard to come by."

When the van pulled up to the cafe, one of the men got out of the van only to see a closed sign on the cafe door. He looked around and saw no one up or down the street.

"Maybe they haven't gotten here yet," the radioman inside the van said to the figure behind him crouched in the back of the van.

The figure in the back looked around carefully and noticed something laying on the ground behind a building a few yards away. "Wrong we didn't get here soon enough. Get back in the van," he commanded the man outside as he jumped out of the van. "Meet me down at that abandoned building." Then he took off running in the direction of the building carrying only his sword. The van had just pulled up as the man got to the body of Doctor Wilson.

One of the men got out of the van. The man in back standing over the body told the other one to call it in. Just then they saw a cop car cruising around the corner. The men jumped into the van, and the van's headlights immediately went out. Slowly they drove behind the building and into an alley and sped away without the cops seeing them.

"Do you see anything, Diana?"

"Not yet," Diana said as she shined the light back and forth over the street. "Are you sure it was your brother's car?"

"I am positive," Darren quickly replied.

"What was your brother doing here?"

"Your guess is as good as mine?"

Then she saw it. "There, over behind the building."

Darren quickly turned the cruiser up into the driveway and jumped out of the car. Diana got out too, but not as fast taking in the scene carefully. She was not about to die tonight.

Darren got to his brother first. "Oh my God!" he shouted. "Oh my God Jerry, Jerry." Darren grabbed his brothers limp and very bloody body.

"Darren!" Diana shouted. "Put him down that's evidence. You are destroying the crime scene."

Darren looked at her with a tear-streaked face and told her to go to hell. Diana ran back to the car and called it in while Darren held his brother's lifeless body in his arms, weeping. It didn't take long for the police and all the other authorities working on the murder case to get there. After some convincing of the other officers on the scene, Darren laid his brother's body down, and slowly walked back to his patrol car. Darren just stood motionless by his patrol car grieving the loss of his brother while Diana stood next to him watching more confusion.

"Do you want me to drive you home?" Diana asked Darren.

"No. I'm okay. I'd rather stay here with him. Besides, they are going to want an escort to the morgue. I'm not going to let his body just disappear as the others did."

There was now a forensics team for the police as well as a forensics team for the D.A.D. working together. When they had worked together before they seemed to get in each other's way and from the looks of things nothing had changed. Everything concerning forensics and records was still a mess. No one had wanted to believe it was anything more than the work of some crazy lunatic or the Red Pack committing the murders, but it was now becoming plain, more organization and a wider perspective were needed. To achieve such a goal, they had to find a way to work together.

"Has anyone found the murder weapon?" Doctor Martin asked of the forensics team for the Chicago Police Department. He asked it as if he knew what the answer might be. He was talking to Doctor Quin the chief of forensics for the northeast region of the FBI

"You sound pretty confident they will find one," Doctor Quin commented. Both men had gotten to the scene almost simultaneously and needed to change from their civilian clothes to the protective clothing which would repel blood. At these scenes, there was always lots of blood.

"I just believe it's all pretty convenient, finding the murder weapon with the detective's fingerprints all over it. A police detective, at that. Don't you think it's a little too obvious?" Dr.

By
J. P. Leonard

Martin asked.

Doctor Quin had already been briefed by the D.A.D. about what they would find. All for national security the D.A.D. had reminded him. The doctor also remembered the briefing he had gotten from his superiors concerning the D.A.D. He had been about twenty minutes early that morning for the briefing and had seen an unusual amount of security there. He had paid it no mind until he saw the man come out of his boss's office. It was the vice-president of the United States. About four Secret Service men were with the vice-president as he stood outside the door shaking his boss's hand. His boss saw him sitting outside the office but didn't acknowledge him until the vice-president was gone. They had exchanged some small talk. His boss had told him about a problem down in Chicago. He had to assist the FBI in doing whatever the FBI wanted.

Quin had asked why did they have to be involved, the FBI had their own people, but his boss had cut him off. In the name of national security, Quin would be asked to do things he ordinarily would not do. "You are a good man, Gerald," his boss said. A patriotic man. I know you won't let me down."

David Neal was surely made a patsy by someone, but who? From where he stood, he knew David Neal could not possibly have been the murderer. Never-the-less he had to play along for his daughter and his job sake.

"I think maybe you have a little too much faith in your fellow man, Quin said to Martin. What's obvious is this Detective David Neal of yours has gone insane. His fingerprints are all over the murder weapons he's been placed at the scene of many of the murders and if we find anything here with his fingerprints on it well—what can you say it's an open and shut case."

Dr. Martin just smiled.

Never Die On A Cold Night II
<u>REVELATIONS</u>

"Are you ready to examine the body?" Dr. Quin asked. He already knew what they would find but for appearance sake, he had to look just as unknowing as Dr. Martin looked.

The next day Sadie talked to David from a telephone booth and arranged to meet him at a residence on the South side of Chicago. It was the home of the now widow of Charley Stilles. Sadie had remembered what David said about his friend and so she had contacted Janet and Janet had agreed to help her. Sadie figured by David seeing an old friend, it might help him to get his memory back. But something had gone wrong. Before Sadie could get out of the office, her boss had come in and told her she had to stay and work with one of the female officers upstairs. Sadie tried to get out of it, but there was no one there who knew computers the way she did. If she just walked out of the precinct, she was afraid someone might get suspicious and maybe catch David. The time for David to meet Sadie at Janet's home was preset. The only way for the time to be changed now was to call David, and she couldn't risk it. She would have to think of something.

David left the inn in a taxi on the way to the address Sadie had given him. She had told him he might see something which might jog his memory. He wanted it to happen more than she did, so he was willing to try most anything. When he got to the address, he saw it was a residential area. There were many apartments on the street. He didn't remember anything. David paid the driver and walked up to the building. Inside the vestibule and found on the wall near the mailboxes the names of the tenants alongside the doorbell and their apartment corresponding apartment numbers. He rang the doorbell.

By
J. P. Leonard

"Yes, can I help you?" A woman said through the intercom.

"Yes, Sadie Phillips asked me to—"

"David, come on up here. You come up here now!"

David heard the buzzer, and he pulled on the second door which was now unlocked and started going up the stairs to Janet's apartment. When he got to the floor her apartment was on, he was greeted by a very pretty woman of color. It was Charley's widow Janet. But David didn't recognize her. Immediately she ran up to him and grabbed him telling him how much she missed him between sobs. He felt for the woman not because he knew her but because of what Sadie had told him about her concerning her husband and her daughter. Now she had no one, and he understood that feeling. He put his arms around her to try and console her.

"I thought you were dead," she said.

"I am very much alive. I just don't know who this guy is that's alive," he said, pointing to himself.

"Let's get out of the hall," she said taking his hand and guiding him into the apartment. "Don't you remember anything?"

"I seem to remember dreams, but that's about it."

While they were talking, there was another ring of her bell.

"I wonder who that could be?" she said as she got up to go to the kitchen intercom. "Yes, can I help you?" she asked the person on the intercom.

"Hi, Mrs. Stilles. My name is George Wentworth. I am with your husband's insurance company." He was really one of the men from the black van who were surveilling Sadie's house. "I was in the area, and I figured I would come over with the last of the paperwork you need to okay, so we can close this case."

"Where is Sidney?" she asked being a little concerned but more annoyed. "He usually sends the papers through the mail."

"That's why I'm here. I was in the area anyway, and Sidney asked me to bring the papers by but if it's too much trouble I could—"

"No, no, just bring them up." she said as she pressed the button to unlock the door.

"It's a shame you don't know who you are talking to," David said.

"Always the detective, David. You do know that's what you are don't you?"

"It's what I've been told."

Janet gave him the once over. "You certainly look the same although you have let your hair grow longer." She paused and sat down in the chair in front of him. She took a long look into David's eyes. "There is something wrong David. Before Charles died, I knew there was something wrong. It's like an evil blanket has come over this town. I get so afraid now; it makes me hate to be alone. I don't know what to do. If only you had your memory." There was a knock and Janet went to open the door.

David watched Janet go to the door. Something about her going to answer the door reminded him of something. He didn't know why he felt troubled and now the feeling of fear was coming back. Janet was opening the door.

"Don't open the door, Janet."

But it was too late. The door flew open knocking Janet to the floor. There was a glass end table next to the door, and she was knocked down hard onto it. David saw her head hit the table and the glass breaking, and then she just lay there. Before he could get up the man aimed a weapon at him. David picked up a pillow and the man fired, a dart into it. David was moving on instinct now. Jumping up from the couch he dived for the man and hit him before the man had a chance to get another shot off. David scrambled to his feet and saw two more men coming through the door at him. The man he had hit lay on the floor, dazed. All three David and the other two men waltzed around the room vicariously waiting for the other to make the first move. As soon as one of the men set both of his feet on a small throw rug David reached down and pulled the rug out from under the man. The man went crashing over the couch onto the floor behind it. The other man kicked David in the head and sent David sprawling backward onto the floor. By that time the man who had the dart gun had refilled it and fired it at David. The dart found it's mark in David's shoulder and the drug acted quickly. All went dark again.

Sadie was sitting next to Trudie at the computer console trying to show her the way to back up all the files in the computer separately because of the computer file thefts. It was something evidently could have been done at another time, but for some reason, it couldn't wait. Sadie had been there too long already. She figured she could make it to Janet's house in about fifteen minutes, so she could still make it to the meeting if she could get out now.

"So, Sadie is this the way you get into the file system by hitting this key over—"

Never Die On A Cold Night II
<u>REVELATIONS</u>

"No! No! That would erase all you have on the disk," Sadie said impatiently. She never liked teaching others, especially those who were slow. But Trudie was a friend, and so she'd have to try to get her to understand.

Trudie pulled her glasses from her eyes and started to rub the corner of her eye.

"What's the matter Trudie something in your eye?" Sadie asked as she set up the program for Trudie.

"Yeah, I think one of my eyelashes went into it. They always get in my eyes. Some women like long eyelashes, but for me, they can be a nuisance."

"Why don't you cut them off?" Sadie said with a smile.

"Very funny," Trudie chuckled out loud.

Sadie turned to her friend and reached up and grabbed Trudie's hand. "Let me see if I can blow it out."

Trudie stepped back. "Not on your life. I'm not going to give these jokers any reason to think I might be a lesbian. They could say we were kissing or something. But if you want to come over to my house for tea then well—" Then Trudie winked at Sadie and headed toward the women's restroom deliberately swinging her bottom provocatively as she walked away.

Sadie was completely taken back by the last comment from her friend. Was she joking or was she serious? If she wasn't joking, she wondered if it would it be unladylike to punch her friend in the mouth. Why would she think such a thing about her? She knew what others were thinking because she didn't sleep around but she thought her friend Trudie would be more understanding.

Sadie started to get mad until she noticed her friend had left her glasses. She remembered her friend saying once she was blind as a bat deprived of her glasses. She looked around slowly to her right and her left. No one was looking at her, so she slowly pushed Trudie's glasses off of the edge of the desk with some computer paper that had been laying on the desk. As soon as the glasses hit the floor Sadie moved her chair, and as if it was an accident, she let the heel of her left shoe step right into one of the lenses, and she heard it crunch beneath her weight. "Oh my God! Trudie's glasses," she said with sincerity. Then she saw Trudie coming back, and she picked the glasses up. Trudie got back to the desk she looked in Sadie's hand and gasped.

"Sadie! I was kidding. You didn't have to break my glasses." Snatching her glasses away from Sadie. "I can't see very well without them."

"Trudie I'm so sorry I didn't do it on purpose," Sadie lied. "It truly was an accident. Look you go right now to your optometrist and get a replacement pair of the glasses. No get two pairs, and I will reimburse you for them—within reason of course."

"I should make you pay for them," Trudie said pouting. "But if you say you didn't do it on purpose, I'll believe you. We will have to finish this later."

Sadie started to gather her coat and things together. "I am sorry Trudie."

"Where are you going Sadie, I thought—"

"Bring me the receipt, Trudie. I trust you. I have to go now," Sadie insisted. "I'll give you the money as soon as you come back with the receipt."

She hollered after Sadie as Sadie hurried down the steps. "I told you; you didn't have to pay for them but if you insist, Sadie I'm going to get it done today."

Never Die On A Cold Night II
<u>REVELATIONS</u>

Sadie agreed and excused herself and got to Janet's apartment fifteen minutes later. She rang the doorbell for a minute but got no answer. Just when she was about to give up a nicely dressed young man opened up the locked door and held it open for her.

"Our landlord is a little cheap. Those old doorbells are always going out, and he takes his own sweet time to fix them I'm afraid. So, come on in I'm sure your friend won't mind. He'll probably be very happy. I know I would be." As Sadie came in, he bowed to the waist as she went by him. "Good day, ma'am."

"Good day, sir," Sadie answered. She hurried to the apartment of Janet Stilles anxious to know if the meeting was truly over or if the young man was right, the doorbell wasn't working. She wanted so much to see David again. Even with all the trouble going on and the fact he didn't remember anything couldn't take away the joy of seeing him and being with him again. When she got to the door, she paused for a moment and stood there, trying to regain her composure. She fussed with her coat and then tossed her hair around to the back and straightened her shoulders. She had it bad, and she knew it. But she still didn't want to seem too obvious. She just barely knocked, and the door began to open at her touch. She pushed the door open wider and what she saw brought terror to her heart. There was blood all over the floor. She walked inside. "David, Janet, where are you?" She had started to run back out of the door when she heard a moan. It was David. There he was, picking himself up off the floor. His white shirt and dark corduroy pants were now covered with blood.

Sadie ran to him and helped him onto the couch. "David, are you all right? Where are you hurt?" She examined his body as she questioned him. David winced as she touched his head. Sadie took away her hand, bloody from where she had touched his head. "You're bleeding."

David pushed himself away and stood up. "Where is she?" he asked. "Where is she? I fought them—there were too many of them. Where is she?"

Sadie noticed the only place David was hurt was the spot on his head. It certainly could not account for all the blood on the floor. David walked out of the room, and she got up to follow him.

"Oh my God!" she heard him shout. "Look at what they did. Oh my God!" David was standing between her and the bedroom, so, at first, she didn't see anything. But peering around him, she saw the headless bloody torso of what might have been Janet. She got sick and ran to the bathroom to vomit. It seemed as if she would never stop. She ran cold water and splashed it on her face. Walking back into the hall again holding the wall as she went, she made it to the bedroom. She no longer saw David standing there. She wondered why she hadn't fainted. Twice she had seen something like this. First Kelly and now Janet. Who could have done such a thing? Walking back into the living room, she saw David sitting on the couch.

"They are going to think I did this Sadie," he said his mouth trembling. "If I had not known what happened I would have believed I did it."

"What happened?"

"She let in her insurance agent. Or at least that's who he said he was, an insurance agent. She let him in from downstairs. I heard everything. When he got upstairs and knocked on the door, I knew something was wrong but before I could stop her, she opened the door and this guy burst through. He shot a dart at me."

"A dart? Why would they do that?"

"To knock me out," he said, looking around. "I held up a pillow. The dart hit the pillow, and now I can't find the dart."

Never Die On A Cold Night II
<u>REVELATIONS</u>

Sadie picked up one of the couch pillows and examined it. Sure enough, there was a very small hole with a wet substance surrounding it. "This must have been the pillow?" Sadie said. David's face brightened at her discovery. "This is like what you said happened before. What are we going to do now David?"

"We have got to get out of here. Did anyone see you come in?"

Sadie remembered the young man. "Yes, someone did."

"Maybe they didn't get a good look at your face."

"I believe he did. But we can't worry about it right now. You've got blood all over you."

"My coat will cover it," he said as he looked around for it. Janet must have put it in the closet. Sadie got up from the couch and went to the closet. "Is this it?" she asked as she pulled it out to show to David.

"Yes."

As Sadie gave the coat to David, she saw a box up on the shelf. She pulled it down and investigated it. There was a gun and ammo in the case. A forty-five automatic. It looked new. "There is a gun here."

"Let me see it."

Sadie handed him the gun.

"I might be able to use this next time." David went to the window and looked out. Across the street, he saw the woman again, the woman he had seen before. This time she was looking up at him gesturing for him to come down. "There is that woman again the one who was in the elevator," he said.

By
J. P. Leonard

Sadie ran to the window and looked down but saw nothing. Before Sadie had gotten to the window, the woman had disappeared before his eyes.

"I don't see her David. Where is she?" Sadie said as she searched his face for a reply.

"She's gone. She just disappeared."

The radio man called the D.A.D.'s headquarters and talked briefly updating the information and waiting for their orders.

"Break off from following them," the D.A.D. commanded. "Let team Fox-trot handle it at this point. Did you call the police?"

"Yes, sir just after they left to make sure they didn't get caught."

"You've done a good job. David will have to come over to our side now; he has nowhere else to go."

"Yes sir" the radioman agreed.

"You have your orders now."

"What about our main subject, the ripper?" the radio man asked.

The D.A.D. thought about it thinking beforehand it could have been David but now he wasn't so sure. "We'll just have to play clean-up until we catch him."

"Yes, sir."

Never Die On A Cold Night II
<u>REVELATIONS</u>

The radio man hung up before the D.A.D. did. But before the Fitzgerald hung up, he heard a click on the line and knew someone was listening. The D.A.D. had not been aware of an intruder. Someone had outsmarted him. But who? Then it dawned on him. Judith O'Brian. How smart she was. It was okay. She was not a threat to his operation. He would deal with her later as he always planned.

That night the air was still and very cold. The sky was void of clouds, so the light of a large, round moon illuminated the buildings around where Trudie lived on the northeast side of Chicago making them look more foreboding than usual. She was trying to hurry home from the store, an all-night convenience store had the kind of stockings she wore to work. The area around where she lived was comprised of mostly decent, hardworking people. The streets were patrolled frequently by the neighborhood police. Tonight, she didn't see anyone. Nothing ever really happened there anyway, so she wasn't bothered about taking a shortcut through an alley.

Halfway through the alley, she heard a growl from just up ahead of her. It sounded like a dog. There were a lot of dogs in the area, and she had come prepared. She reached into her coat pocket and took out a can of mace which boosted her courage tremendously.

"All right, you mangy old mutt come on out of there. Come and get your mace, my friend," she said gleefully. She wanted it to come out. She would spray the heck out of it. She kept walking until she came up to the place in the alley where she thought the sound came. It was a corner of the alley where two buildings came together. Part of the alley was very dark, but she knew something, or someone was there. She could almost see the shadow of a man or something. Looking up the alley she could see the street about fifty feet away. It looked like a thousand to her. She remembered something her father had said before she would go to sleep if you think you see a monster, go up and hit it. Chances are it was only a toy or the way your clothes looked at the back of the chair or your eyes playing tricks on you. You must face your fears he had told her. And she always did. This time was no different than any other. She had to face her fears.

Trudie started to walk closer to the shadow gripping her mace in her hands. She moved with deliberateness. She was only ten feet from the shadow, and the area started to smell very foul, so much so she covered her nose with her free hand. The closer she got to the shadow the more afraid she became. Her heart was beating loudly in her ears. Her breath came in short gasps. She had never been so afraid in her life. Why did she do what her father said? It was not the cozy bedroom of her own house; this was an alley. Like the alleys where people wound up dead. Something in her head told her to run with all the speed she could muster but she couldn't. Her legs would not move.

Whatever was in the darkness let out a growl so deep and loud it made the ground quake under her feet, and the smell intensified. The growl seemed to unlock her legs and made her turn to run. It was too late. It was as if someone had hit her in the back with a sledgehammer. The blow she felt lifted her body about three feet off the ground, and she seemed to fly through the air to the wall of the building across the alley. She hit the wall with so much force that it dazed her for a moment but not enough not to see the monster standing over her, salivating from its dog-like mouth. It was hideous as it stood over her dazed body. It waited for a moment. She knew she would die.

CHAPTER ELEVEN

"Remember the Gods are at work here."

In another part of the city a wearied D.A.D. Fitzgerald was getting news of another murder. He swore when he heard the news. "How long are we going to be in the dark concerning this guy? My lord have chosen this for me. I have no idea who—or what—he is." He was silent for a minute.

"Obviously the evidence you keep planting is not going to keep working," Dr. Quin said. "Some smart lab technician is going to spot—"

"Your job is not to spot the obvious," the D.A.D. said. "Yours is to obey. Isn't that right?"

The doctor hesitated for a moment. He was not used to being ordered so harshly. "Yes, Sir you are right. But do you mind if I ask you something? Are you religious? You said the lord left you in the dark what did you mean by that?"

"Ah, doctor you do ask too many questions. Maybe in time,

you may get some answers." And with his reply, the D.A.D. left the room.

The next morning at the Third Precinct an argument involving the captain and a small group of people was taking place in the refreshment lounge.

"Darn machine," Officer Belcher spat out as she tried to get her morning caffeine fix from the candy machine. It was the second quarter she had lost in two days. "Somebody is going to have to do something about this machine."

No one was listening. Sadie Phillips and Doctor Martin were trying to convince the captain to look elsewhere for the murderer while the captain was seemly trying to evade the whole issue.

"So, you won't look at the evidence?" the doctor asked captain Edwards.

"I've already seen the evidence," the captain replied.

"Not this evidence" Sadie said. "This new evidence states someone placed the fingerprints on all these murder weapons."

"Why don't you stop trying to convince me someone else committed those murders. That murderer David Neal placed his fingerprints on the weapon when he used it to kill the coroner."

"We don't believe that's true, captain," the Doctor replied.

"All you have is the conjecture of one lab assistant," the captain said.

"But there is also physical evidence," Dr. Martin insisted.

Never Die On A Cold Night II
REVELATIONS

"There is putty, or traces of it on the so-called murder weapon. The same type of material you would find plumbers use. If you have a fingerprint, you wish to lift you can do it using that putty and then, in theory, take the same material and use it to make fake prints and place it on another object and it will leave that same fingerprint only traces of the putty will remain as well. It's what we believe has happened with the murder weapons we have been finding in the area of the murder sites."

"But is there any concrete proof this is what happened?" the captain asked.

They shook their heads no.

"Then there you have it. I think you two are beating a dead horse."

Just then the heated discussion in the squad room was interrupted by an unannounced visitor. It was a man in a black suit wearing a white collar around his neck and a chain around his neck with a gold crucifix. Most of the eyes in the squad room were on the priest as he walked up to captain Edwards. "I am Father Mallonee."

"Yes, Father, can I help you?" captain Edwards asked with a smile.

"Maybe but I don't believe you will. Whether by choice or by ignorance."

Captain Edwards screwed his face up with a puzzled look. "I'm sorry?"

Sadie was also puzzled by the statement of the priest, and so was dr. Martin. But the doctor had a previous engagement and told Sadie he would see her later. Walking out the door of the detective's squad room he gave the priest one last glance and then left.

"There is a young man a very dear friend of mine who works here. His name is David Neal."

The captain had been interested in what the priest wanted until he spoke of David Neal. "I am truly sorry, Father, but he isn't here. As a matter of fact, there is a search going on for him right now. When we hear something, you will be one of the first to know. Now if you will excuse me, I—"

"Such a pitiful shame," the priest said. "David talked of you all as being his family. His friends to the end, he said as he spoke of you, but I see it is not so. Nevertheless, I can help you. I know David has not done the things he is accused."

The captain stopped to listen to what Father Mallonee had to say. "Do you have any proof, Father?"

"Yes, but not any you will believe," he said not cracking a smile. "But if you will allow me, I can help you find the real murderer."

"Tell me, sir, how do you expect to do this?"

"With God's help, of course," the priest said matter-of-factly.

"Well sir, I'm sorry, but I can't jeopardize the safety of citizens by allowing them to be involved in police business."

"As I said I would find no help here," the priest said. "When I find out I will supply you with the information. Then it will be up to you to act on it."

"If you have something, sir, we will be happy to look into it," captain Edwards replied coolly and walked away. Father Mallonee also started to walk away, but before he could get down the steps, Sadie went after him.

"Father Mallonee," Sadie called out.

Father Mallonee turned around. "Yes."

"I know it may seem David has a shortage of friends around here, but I am a friend of his."

"Then maybe we should talk. You have me at a disadvantage. What is your name?"

"Forgive me Father I—my name is Sadie Phillips."

She held out her hand to him.

"I am pleased to make your acquaintance Miss Phillips?"

"You can call me Sadie. "

"All right, Sadie. You said you are a friend of David's?"

"Yes, very much so. David asked me to marry him," Sadie said happily.

"You don't know how happy I am to hear this Sadie, but I wish he had been here to tell me himself." He looked at Sadie's puzzled look. "Not that I don't believe you I do. You seem to speak things from the heart, and most people don't. I believe you. It's just I miss him. It's been a while since I last saw him."

"Father, are you hungry?"

"I think I could eat something."

"There is a cafeteria not too far from here. We can talk, and I can buy you lunch."

"Sure, why not. Besides I hate to refuse a good friend of David's and such a pretty one.

"Okay then let me get my coat, and I'll meet you at the front desk." When Sadie returned, they went together to the cafeteria. On the way there they briefed each other on their knowledge of David. They both had information to give. Sadie didn't tell the priest she knew where David was.

Finally, they were both sitting at the table when the waitress came over.

"Would you like for me to take your order now?"

"Could we have a couple of minutes please?" Sadie asked the waitress.

"Sure, ma'am. My name is Katy," she said with a slightly southern accent. "I'll leave you with these menu's and bring you some coffee and water to drink while you wait, if you like."

"That will be fine, Katy." Sadie turned back to the priest. "Father you said David had come to see you not long ago. You said the conversation you had concerned you. Can I ask what you talked about?"

"I'm afraid David is in some real trouble. I have been tracking these murders the police can't seem to find the answers to, and they resemble something I read about in a library in Paris. Are you a Catholic, Miss Phillips? I'm sorry—Sadie."

"That's ok Father. No, I'm not Catholic," she said looking down.

"Are you religious in any way?" he asked very sincerely. "I'm sorry, I didn't mean to put you on the spot. It's just what I am about to tell you—well—"

Never Die On A Cold Night II
REVELATIONS

"I do go to church but not very often, so I do believe in God," she said defensively. "And I know I'll make David a good wife."

"I'm sure you will I didn't mean to insinuate any—"

Just then the waitress came back. "I'm not trying to rush you, folks; you take your time now. Here are your coffee and two glasses of water. Just call me if you need anything."

"We need just a little more time miss," he said. She nodded and smiled, then left them alone. The priest turned back to Sadie. "The reason why I asked you if you were religious was basically to find out how much you know about the bible?"

"Not very much, Father but go on."

"You see, it kind of ties into the murders. Let me just let you read something."

He reached into his briefcase and pulled out a very old King James Bible and turned to a certain part and handed it to Sadie. "Please, read the scriptures I have highlighted before I go on."

Sadie took the bible from him as if it were a rare and delicate relic placed it on the table directly in front of her and began to read.

While the word was in the king's mouth there fell a voice from heaven saying O king Neb-u-Chad-Nez'-zar to thee it is spoken; The kingdom is departed from thee. And they shall drive thee from men and thy dwelling shall be with the beasts of the field: they shall make thee to eat grass as oxen and seven times shall pass over thee until thou know the most High ruleth in the kingdom of men and giveth it to whomso-ever he will. The same hour was the thing fulfilled upon Neb-u-chad-Nez'-zar; and he was driven from men and did eat grass as oxen and his body was wet with the dew of heaven till

his hairs were grown like eagles' feathers and his nails like birds' claws.

Sadie lifted her head and the priest searched her face for a sign to show she understood but her face only exhibited bewilderment.

"Do you understand what you have read?"

"I'm not sure? This Neb-u-chad-Nez'-zar was a king?"

"Yes."

"And he went crazy...or at least I think that's what the scripture is saying. You tell me, Father, you're the expert."

"No one is an expert, but I will give you a couple of observations. The writer has written about the takeover of the children of Israel by the Babylonian Empire. According to the writer God caused this to happen. But the king God used to do it Neb-u-chad-Nez'-zar got lifted up in himself and started to boast of what he had done, because he defeated many great nations, as well as the nation of Israel. According to the writer God got angry and took away the man's human mind and gave him the mind of an animal."

"Kind of fantastic, isn't it, father?"

"It gets better. This man believed himself to be an animal so much, so he began to look like one. His hair got longer his nails got longer, and I imagine he did look pretty wild. In those days superstition ran rampant and anybody believing they were possessed by some animal or some spirit might actually believe they were changing into that animal or spirit."

"Do you mean like the movies I saw as a child—a werewolf or something?" Sadie asked. All the while she was trying to keep from laughing. "Do you really believe that kind of thing can happen to somebody?"

"Sadie I am a psychiatrist as well as a priest. I have seen some very extraordinary things. I have observed patients who believed they were animals but I have never seen one physically change. Although you can't discount the possibility."

As Sadie's thoughts of David and his predicament flooded back into her mind, the humor she felt behind what Father Mallonee said concerning monsters and werewolves went away. A look of seriousness was in her eyes as she spoke to him. "Father before you go on, I have to tell you something," she said lowering her voice. "I know where David is, but he has amnesia."

"Can you take me to him, Sadie?"

"It's not safe for David. Someone is following me."

"I understand."

"But I can send you to him."

After Sadie and Father Mallonee decided how to get Father Mallonee to David's hotel, Sadie contacted David and told him the complete plan. David wanted very much to see Father Mallonee although he didn't remember the priest. They both agreed the priest might be able to help restore his memory, it was worth the risk of the priest visiting him.

Sadie left the restaurant hoping the people following her would not follow the priest. If they did, however, the priest would take them on a wild goose chase, and when it was safe, he would go straight to the hotel.

Finally, when he arrived at the hotel, he had decided he would wear civilian clothes. No one needed to know he was a priest.

By
J. P. Leonard

He stood for a moment looking into a store window at his reflection trying to remember the last time he had worn civilian clothes. It felt strange. But not as strange as the evening felt. He had only been standing there for a few minutes, and already it was starting to get dark.

CHAPTER TWELVE

"The stories told"

Night came quickly after the sun had started to go down. It hadn't been much sun anyway. The clouds had shielded it. But there were no clouds tonight. They had all but disappeared which left the city very cold. Deadly cold. The wind chill made the temperature feel like forty below zero although the real temperature was ten degrees. The cold and harsh blowing wind caused his eyes to water as he stared at the large white moon. He didn't mind the cold. The cold was inconsequential. What did matter was he knew there would be another murder and the fact he would be with David would help to prove David did not kill those people. Father Mallonee took one last look at the streets before going into the hotel. They were deserted, and rightly so. It would seem not many people would want to brave this cold. Only people concerned for others might do it—and, of course, any lunatic with a purpose.

The priest gave two hard knocks on the door, paused, and then gave three more. It was the signal they had agreed upon so David went to the door and opened it.

Father Mallonee spoke first because he knew David would probably not recognize him. He knew he had to go easy at this first meeting. "Hello David, I'm Father Mallonee. How are you Son?"

"I'm fine won't you come in. Will you need something to drink?"

"Hot tea..." He paused. "Never mind you wouldn't remember I drink only tea made with real tea leaves and occasionally cold milk."

"It's no trouble I can call up room service," David replied as he started to pick up the phone.

"No, David. Please sit down." The priest went over to the couch. "There are a lot of important things we must accomplish, and one of them is my examination of you. So, if you will please come here and sit down."

David walked over to the couch and sat down. "Will Sadie be coming soon?"

"You and Sadie like each other." the priest said, in

more of a statement than a question He started to feel David's head for indications of a blow.

"I don't know. Ouch!" David winced with pain as the priest touched a sore spot on the back of David's head.

"The way you two act I would say so. That's tender where I placed my finger, I presume?" he said as he touched the tender spot again.

Never Die On A Cold Night II
<u>REVELATIONS</u>

David winced again.

"There is something there, David, and I can't see in this light."

"There is a brighter light in the bathroom. What do you think it is?"

"I don't know, but we will find out. I am a medical doctor as well as a psychiatrist, but I don't practice the medical part of it. However, I do know what I'm doing." He motioned for David to accompany him to the bathroom. "Please, let's get into some better light."

Inside the bathroom, he could see David's scalp better, and what he saw alarmed him. "David, I know why you can't remember anything now. Whoever did this is very good. I mean exceptionally good. There are not many men who can do this, but then there are not many men who would do it even if they could because it is against the law."

"What are you talking about, what do you think is wrong? What did someone do to me?"

"I don't mean to alarm you David, but I like to have my patients understand the problems they are having and why they have them." He took hold of David's arm and brought him out of the bathroom setting him down on the couch. He took a chair from a nearby table and sat it in front of David. He looked straight into David's eyes. "Someone has surgically induced you into a state of amnesia. It was not a blow on the head as I had first thought might have happened. Neither was it by any type of stress which could have been another possibility. Someone had surgically placed electrodes to your brain and blocked your memories of your past life."

"Can the process be reversed?"

"Yes, yes it can. But it can also be very dangerous."

"Tell me the truth Father you have so far. Don't stop now."

"Well like I said it can be reversed. In theory, all you have to do is cut the wires—"

"Wires?"

"Yes. There are two wires in the back of your head with the appearance of strands of hair. Those imposter strands of wire are connected to another short strand which is actually a transmitter. It's all brilliant I tell you; whoever did this. The impulses from the small transmitter travel across these wires to the brain. Cutting those wires, in theory, will stop the signals to the brain which is causing the block to your long-term memory and you should start remembering everything."

"How do you know what you're looking at isn't wires at all but my hair?"

"Your hair is black isn't it David?"

"Yes, sir it is."

"Well, the imitation hair, or shall I say wires, and electrical component is brown and very strong I might add." Father Mallonee got up from the chair and had David to move so he could see the back of his head. There was a lamp there, so he removed the shade to have more light to see. When he found the wires, he pulled on them gently.

"Ouch," David said, for the pain. "So, what is the dangerous part?"

"You could lose all control of your mental abilities."

Never Die On A Cold Night II
REVELATIONS

"You mean I could lose my mind?"

"Or the equivalent. Plus, all memory could be lost forever.
And I mean all of it. Your mind could revert to a baby's and
would have to learn everything all over again."

David then sat back on the couch and stared at the floor for a
long while.

"So, you have two choices David," the priest stated calmly.
"One, to stay as you are and protect the transmitter as best as you
can until it turns off by itself or two, let me disconnect it now and
face the possibility of living in an insane asylum for the rest of
your life."

The priest thought for a minute. "You might want to consider
Sadie before you do it. That is, if you decide to do it."

"I can't consider Sadie father I don't remember her or how we
felt about each other. The problem is this thing could go out at
any time am I right? But you could cut the wires, and I could get
my memory back, or I could go insane either way?"

"Yes, to all three questions David," the priest agreed. "So,
whatever you decide I will go along with it, and whatever
happens I will be with you."

David got up from the couch and walked over to the small bar
and fixed himself a drink in silence. He stood silent and very still
for the space of about two or three minutes. Then he put the
glass to his lips and drank the fiery hot liquid down in one gulp,
wincing as it went down his throat. It was very warm and
comforting in his belly which helped him to make his decision.
"Let's do it, father." He then walked into the bathroom.

"I'll need some scissors or something which will cut well."

By
J. P. Leonard

David searched through the medicine cabinet only to find a fingernail clipper. "Can you use this?"

"I think so." The priest took the clippers from David's hand. "Are you ready?"

"I am if you are."

Father Mallonee lifted the hair covering the transmitter revealing the two wires going into his head. He placed the clipper cutting-edge completely around both the wires and waited. "It is going to cut well, David, and I am cutting…now." The clipper cut right through the wires and the transmitter fell down the back of David's shirt. The priest took it and put it in his pocket. "How do you feel David?"

"I feel—" David's speech was cut off abruptly by a barrage of sensations coursing through his body—or his mind he couldn't tell which. Then the images started to flow through his mind, all kinds of images from his life; some from dreams he'd had from his past experiences. They were all so confusing. In the background, he could hear the priest's voice or what sounded like the priest. The images were coming so fast he blacked out completely. When he came to, he was lying on the couch in the hotel room. Father Mallonee was sitting across from him, and he remembered who Father Mallonee was as well as who he was. David smiled. "Hello, Father I remember everything."

"I am glad son. I'm glad," the priest said, smiling.

The two men both hugged one another and cried. David remembered everything even the dreams he had as a child. Some of the dreams seemed very real, but he knew they had to be dreams because they were out of place as far as his real life was concerned. He remembered Sadie and the love he had for her, but he also remembered where he was and what the Red Pack did to him. He began to tell Father Mallonee everything, all that happened to him from the last time he had seen him and the priest believed him.

Then Father Mallonee began to tell David about his extraordinary observations of what he thought might be going on. He told him of a story that was true. David listened attentively. "David, I have found sometimes when one is confronted by real life all the education one have received can be useless. The advice I have for you, I am afraid, you won't take, but I am going to give it to you regardless of how you feel."

"I think I know what you are going to say, and you are probably right, but with all due respect your type of life is not for me."

"Then life is not for you. If you don't take my advice, then I will try to give you some information that may help you. There are some papers on the occult I found in an old archive in Paris where I was studying. The papers explained how the church tried to keep certain diabolic events from the public. The priest and cardinals who were involved were sent to live out the rest of their lives in a sanctuary for a priest who had been weakened from fighting with the devil. In other words, they were put into an insane asylum."

"What was it that caused them to go crazy?"

"That is not a word we use. Instead, we would rather say delusional, but they were neither. But to go on, the priest were not sent there because of their sanity but for their silence and safety. It all started in Italy during the Second World War. A young German soldier decided to defect. But he had been thinking about his wife and children and didn't want to desert his friends. However, he knew the war was a mistake, and he could not deal with it anymore. Finally, after biding his time he saw a chance to escape. So that night he left his friends and ran through the forest not knowing what sinister things would befall him. He wanted to defect to the Americans as so many of them did. The map he was following did not give him the bearings he needed to get to the front lines or at least the front lines where there was less fighting and more surrendering, but he kept going anyway."

David leaned forward with interest.

"After a while, he knew he was lost. Looking around the area, he saw a brook and a nice grassy knoll to lay on he was quite tired and needed to rest. Getting close to the brook was a little tricky seeing it was down a slope. He had to use his rifle to get down to the brook without falling, so holding the rifle by the butt, he let the rifle barrel dig into the ground while he held on to it to keep from slipping. After he made his way down to the water, he knelt-down and scooped up some into his hand. The first handfuls he splashed over his face and the back of his neck. The next handful he drank. Although it was only May, it was pretty warm. Way off in the distance, he heard what sounded like the howl of wolves. He turned to see where they were coming from but couldn't see a thing. After listening for a while, he decided he must have heard dogs, so he laid himself down on the soft grass and went to sleep."

"Just before dawn, he was awakened by the sound of howling again. This time it sounded like it was coming from no more than a fifth of a kilometer away. Reaching for his rifle, he got to his feet. Because of the slope he either had to raise his weapon and be ready to fire it or climb the slope to see what was there. He chose the first. So, he stood with his weapon cocked and ready trembling as the howling came closer. Then the howling became growls. He had never heard a wolf before let alone seen one. The growls of the wolves terrified him. He remembered the tales, of how they sometimes attacked humans."

David was gripping the arms of his chair now, anxious to hear the rest.

Never Die On A Cold Night II
REVELATIONS

"He was not a coward the soldier thought to himself. He would still be in the war if it hadn't been for that crazy lunatic killing all those Jews. His wife was Jewish. He had protected them by sending them to Switzerland even before he had heard his countrymen were killing Jews. All the thoughts had taken his mind off the danger steadily coming closer, but now the growling and howling had stopped. The sun was now coming up. It was light now, and he needed to be on his way. As he reached the top of the slope, he saw two little girls one about six and the other about nine or ten. They were standing about ten feet away from him. They were both dressed in what appeared to be some animal skins and they just stood there holding each other's hands and watching him. After hesitating for a moment or two, he started to walk towards them to question them. They looked at each other and took off running into the forest. 'Little girls little girls I'm not going to hurt you,' he shouted to them. He started running after them. He needed to find out where he was, and the children could probably help him. But the children were too fast for him. How could they get away so quickly? He figured if he kept going in a straight line, eventually he would reach the end of woods. After going about two miles he was convinced he must have gone deeper into the woods, he was lost. He needed to get his bearings, so he looked for the sun, but the trees were hiding it. He started walking, trying to find enough clearing where he could see it, but by the time he saw the sun it had started going down again. After going so far, he saw inside a very large clearing what was a small cottage nicely kept but in the middle of nowhere. It must have been where the children went the soldier thought. As he got closer to the house, he heard a woman singing. He could not understand what she was singing because he didn't understand Italian, but it was very beautiful. It was as if the singing had drawn him to her. When he got to the house, he noticed the singing wasn't coming from inside the house but from behind it. As he walked around the house, he happened to look through one of the circle-shaped windows and saw the two little girls staring at him and giggling to each other. The singing got louder, so he decided to investigate. Turning and walking to the back of the house he was pleasantly surprised to see a beautiful woman bathing in a very large metal tub. She was the most beautiful woman he had ever seen in his life. So beautiful it took his breath away."

"This is beginning to sound like a romance novel Father," David said teasingly.

"This is supposed to be a true story," the priest emphasized. "And it is far from being a romantic novel. According to this true account although he was standing there in plain view of the woman being speechless the woman never acknowledged his presence in any way or even looked at him. The woman started to get out of the tub, and the young soldier quickly turned around, as not to embarrass her. He seemed to be more embarrassed than she was. He started telling her with his back to her what his troubles were. About his family, the army, and everything. While he was telling her his story, he heard a growl so loud and so deep the very ground where he was standing quaked from the vibration. All this time he had the rifle in his hand. Instinctively he turned around and fired his weapon, and the barrel exploded. He had not cleaned the gun since he had used it as support to get down to the brook. The gun was useless, but the firing of it stunned what had been behind him thus giving him a chance to look at it. He described it as being about ten feet tall. It had a very large head like the head of a lion and the mouth of a ferocious dog with huge fangs coming out of it. The body was completely covered with hair like a bear. The legs and arms were very thick and huge, and the stench was over-powering. He said the worst part about the beast was its eyes. They were as big as saucers and bloodshot red, and they seemed to paralyze its victim with its stare."

David's face had paled.

Never Die On A Cold Night II
REVELATIONS

"What's the matter?" Father Mallonee asked.

David was silent for a while. "I have had dreams or visions—I don't know what. But I have seen this thing. And when I think about it, I think I have seen this forest and cabin. I know this sounds crazy, but I've been there—at least in my dreams."

"There are many unexplained phenomena, David, things which can't readily be substantiated or explained away. I believe I can understand your frustration. But let me tell you the rest of this story it may give us the answers we are looking for."

David nodded.

"The soldier knew he would die or believed he would. He could see no way of escape. The beast was about ten feet away from him but before the man could think his next thought the beast ran upon him with so much speed that it appeared to be in two places at one time. He looked at the beast's mouth. It was now bleeding or had blood on its mouth. 'Oh my God!' he said, even though he didn't believe in God. 'It's blood.' While the beast seemed to toy with him, he felt a searing pain in his chest. He looked down and saw he was bleeding badly from his chest. The beast must have bitten right through his clothes and ripped the flesh from his now bloody chest in one quick move. By then the soldier, being weak from his wound fell to the ground. He knew it was the end now, but he didn't think of himself. He thought only of his wife and two children. What would they do with him gone?

Suddenly and without warning, there was a crack of thunder or what sounded like thunder and the beast ran away in fear. Before the soldier fainted from his wound, he saw what appeared to be a man dressed in a black hooded robe with a golden whip in his hand coming towards him. The soldier said he didn't know if he was dreaming or if he was awake. As the man came near the sound of the golden whip dragged on the ground sounded like a

By
J. P. Leonard

hundred metal chairs being dragged across a cement floor all at one time.

When the soldier regained consciousness, he found himself inside of the cabin laying on one of the three beds. He was on the larger one in the corner of the room. Someone had bandaged him, and his chest felt a hundred percent better. He figured he must have been there for days. There was a man dressed in black clothes with long black hair just as handsome as the woman had been beautiful. The man sat there with a smile on his face. The woman was sitting at a table in the middle of the floor with the children sitting around the table, and all three were looking very sad. 'Where is the beast?' the soldier asked the man sitting next to him.

'Living among us,' the man had replied. The soldier tried to raise himself as much as the pain would let him look, to see his savior.

'What's that supposed to mean?' the soldier asked portraying a look of puzzlement. 'Why the strange answer?'

'Don't worry about the beast' the man in black said. Nether is my answer strange. I have a proposition for you.'

The solder was very grateful for the man's help, and he wanted to repay the man, so he told him as soon as he was able to get out of the forest and he got to his bank in Switzerland he would send him a generous reward.

'That won't be necessary, but there is something you can do. You can mate with this woman.'

The solder was outraged and painfully jumped up from the bed. 'I won't do it. Isn't that your wife?'

The man laughed and assured him she was not his wife.

Never Die On A Cold Night II
<u>REVELATIONS</u>

'That's not all we want you to do. The woman is sometimes human and other times a wolf. We want you to be one as well.'

The agitated movement caused the solder to become weak again, and he had to be helped by the man back into bed."

"How do you remember so much about the story, Father?"

"I guess you forgot, I have a photographic or eidetic memory. I read the whole conversation memorized it and never forgot it. You see the man's confession was put on paper after the whole story was placed on tape. Both paper and tape transcription were locked away. Now stop interrupting and listen."

David nodded.

'You will do what I have proposed,' the man told the soldier.

'What makes you think I will do such a thing?'

The man smiled. 'I have your wife and daughters. Just as I have this man's wife and daughters'

"With that, the man in black disappeared. The soldier didn't know what to say about what the man said, nor about the man just disappearing before his eyes. He never saw the man again neither did he see the beast again. However, he did get to know the woman and her children well. She helped him to get better and never touched him in a sexual way. He never mentioned to her about the man he saw or the beast. He figured a wolf probably bit him, but considering the rest he'd seen, he tried to convince himself he must have been hallucinating, so he never mentioned it. And neither did she. As soon as he was better, the woman brought him to where he needed to go to defect to the Americans. He helped the Americans locate many of the Germans' whereabouts because he figured they would surrender and they did. The Americans found they could trust him and he was finally allowed to go to his wife and children. Although he had not contacted them, he had sent them away with plenty of money, enough for about five years so they should have been okay. It had been four years since he'd last seen his family, and about three and a half years since he'd last seen the woman and children in the woods. The war was about over, and now he would see his family.

"When he got to Switzerland, he didn't find his wife and children where they were supposed to be. The real estate agent that had arranged the purchase of the house said his wife lived there for only a month. He had gone there to bring her some money from the negotiations, and they were gone. The only thing left was a note addressed to the soldier. All it said was," 'Darling, please come get us we are with him.' Immediately he remembered the man in black and what he had said. After he checked the bank for the money, he found all the money was still there except for one month's withdrawal.

"The soldier took off for Italy and the cabin in the woods there. When he got there, the man in black was waiting. He told the man if he didn't tell him where his wife and children were, he would kill him. The man in black only laughed, and it made the soldier furious. He charged the man, but before he got to him, the man disappeared and reappeared in another spot but always near the soldier. After the second try, the soldier didn't want to believe it, but he came to realize the man was not human. Then the man told him the proposition again. Reluctantly the soldier agreed to it.

That night in the presence of a full moon and in the presence of the woman and her children, the man in black gave him an ointment of some type and a belt made of wolf's hair. He told the soldier he had to apply this ointment all over his completely nude body put the belt on, stand in the middle of a strange circle and read aloud a poem given him. The man in black assured him he would have his wife and children back as soon as his demands were met. The soldier agreed to it and did as the man in black had commanded and had sex with the woman. To the soldier's surprise and shame, he enjoyed it as much as he did with his wife. Then, with the woman's help, he rubbed the ointment all over his body and put the belt on. He stood inside the circle and recited the poem. That night, the soldier turned into a replica of the beast he had seen the first time. As the beast, he had the mind of a beast yet the intelligence of a man. He went into a village and killed three people that night and drank their blood.

"The next day the soldier was sick to his stomach at what he had done. He sat on the edge of the bed in the cottage with his head in his hands. Then he heard a familiar voice. 'Honey are you all right?' He raised his head to find only the woman staring at him. 'Where is she?' the soldier asked as he ran out of the cabin and looked around frantically searching for the person who had just spoken to him. The woman came to the door of the cabin and called out to him. He knew his wife's voice, but this woman was not his wife. The voice, however, did sound just like his wife. She began to tell him her memory of him had been taken away until after he had turned into the beast. When she told him intimate details of their knowledge of each other, he realized she and the children were his. Then as if by some miracle she was not a strange woman anymore. By looks and by speech she was his wife. The soldier shouted with happiness as he grabbed his wife. When he saw his children, he knew them as his own, as they also recognized him as their father and ran to him and wept. Then his two children started to sound strange. He backed away from them only to find they were starting to go through a metamorphosis. He tried to talk to them as his wife looked on in horror, but it was to no avail. The children as wolves would not listen to their father. He thought the only way to control them was as the wolf and he allowed himself to change. But as the wolf he was a murderer and being much stronger then the children, he killed the oldest and drank her blood, but the youngest got away. After his wife saw him that way and saw what happened, she too changed into a wolf, and they fought each other. The husband, being the stronger, soon overcame her, and he murdered her as well drinking her blood. After his ravenous hunger and desire for blood was filled, he quickly changed back into his human form sat down on the ground and wept all that day into the evening. He searched all the night for his daughter but never found her, and soon he gave up the desperate hunt.

David looked at him with wide eyes. "And?"

The father went on. "The next day according to the soldier the man in black visited him again and told him there was a way to get back to being human permanently. Not only would he be a man, but he would be immortal. All he had to do was to kill twelve humans. All of the locations had to be at least one mile away from the other, and all the victim's locations together had to create the form of a pentagram. The murders had to take place during the winter months of one year, and he gave him explicit details on how to accomplish the murders. Those murders David, were the same as the murders committed this year."

"You do know even though I have had these dreams this is truly hard to believe. Let's say for argument's sake all you have said was true. Where is this guy? What do you think has happened to him?"

"The Catholic Church is very discreet in these matters. They would never come out and confess these things are true. Through some connections I have, I found out the man eventually ended up in an insane asylum in a monastery in England. Two priests found him in Cambodia during their travels. They took the man with them. They felt they could help him and they thought it would make good ties between the Church and the Cambodian people."

Never Die On A Cold Night II
<u>REVELATIONS</u>

"Wait a minute, you said the man was taken from Cambodia. How long was he there?"

"I believe over twenty years."

"Is he still there? At the monastery?"

"No, he died. It was said he escaped back to Cambodia and there he was killed. Before he died, he kept in contact with the two priests, but in 'sixty-seven he was killed. Some say the Viet Cong some say the Americans. I don't know."

"I know, Father," David said. He remembered what Hanniz had told him. "My God I know."

"What? Not that it matters. He was an abomination he had to die. But do you think you know something concerning his death?"

"We did it." David got up from the couch he had been sitting.

"The Americans my division we did it."

"Are you sure?"

"I'm positive. Hanniz told me."

"Who is Hanniz?"

"He is the leader of a terrorist group calling themselves the Red Pack. He is also the murderer responsible for the deaths of many people and friends I know. They are the ones who kidnapped me. Hanniz knew I was in that division. He knew everything about me and he told me what we did was ordered by the government. He found out it wasn't a mistake that killed those civilians, that it was supposed to happen. However, he didn't seem to know the reason for their deaths." David shivered.

"Now I know why. The government must have known about the man and had him killed. Maybe the whole camp was full of werewolves." David thought about it and laughed aloud. "What am I saying? I don't believe in werewolves. Do you father?"

"I don't discount anything unless I can prove it isn't true."

"Hanniz also wanted me to join him and his gang."

"Why would he want that, David? What's so special about you joining him?"

"I don't know, but I am here now. What they tried didn't work. Thanks to you."

"No, thanks to God! The other question is why they would go to all that trouble to erase your memory?"

David shrugged and sat back on the couch. "I don't know that either."

The priest sat back in his chair as well. After a while, the priest sat up. "They are going to try to kidnap you again. When I think about it, it makes perfect sense. If you had continued to have amnesia, you would have been picked up by the police. They might have let you stay in jail until you were convicted. Most probably that is when they would have re-captured—or shall I say rescued you. Then, when they asked you to join them again, you might not have been so quick to refuse, seeing they would have been all you had."

"I wouldn't have joined the rat if death was facing me."

"Maybe not and then on the other hand, maybe you would have joined him just to clear yourself."

"He is a murderer. He killed Patricia Hills the motel owner,

Never Die On A Cold Night II
REVELATIONS

Charley, Janet, Nicola and Charley's daughter Theresa and whoever else I do not know."

"He didn't kill all of them, David. Not the people who had been ripped up. It would be the work of another murderer."

"Don't tell me," David said sarcastically. "It's the work of the werewolf. Besides, I thought you said the German was dead?"

"What about the village?"

"No one could have escaped from the village. We made sure of it. We surrounded the village and placed explosive charges around the perimeter. Then we threw a kind of poisonous gas inside, and most of them died instantly. The others were blown up or shot as we saw them come out. But they would have died eventually from the gas we threw in there even if we hadn't shot them or blown them up."

"Such a terrible thing for the people David but I believe you suffered as well."

"I did but not as much as those people. I still hear them sometimes screaming at night when everything is quiet, even though they are all dead."

"Then it leaves only one-person David, the man's daughter. She may still be alive. Or if she's not, she could have infected someone else."

There was a knock on the door. It was the knock Sadie had given David while he had amnesia. David remembered it and went to the door cautiously opening. It was Sadie and no one else. David didn't want Sadie to know he remembered her just then; he wanted to surprise her. As Sadie came through the door she kept her eyes on David. "Even when she walked into the living room, and didn't acknowledge the priest.

By
J. P. Leonard

The priest cleared his throat.

"Oh, I'm sorry, Father I didn't mean to ignore you. How are you? How are things going?"

"I'm fine. I can understand you are preoccupied. I was trying to get someone else to tell you before I do."

"Tell me what?" She said excited. "Come on David tell me what? You don't have your memory back, do you?"

David nodded.

"Oh my God! David you're alright?"

"Yes," David said happily. "I remember everything."

Sadie ran to David and threw herself into his arms covering his face with kisses.

The priest cleared his throat again. "I know you two are happy, but I haven't heard any wedding bells yet.

"Don't worry, Father just as soon as this is all over with, we'll be married," David said, looking into Sadie's eyes, and smiling. Then David's eyes got serious, and the smile left his face. "We have a weightier matter Sadie. Father Mallonee believes a werewolf maybe the reason for the deaths of those people."

Sadie turned around to face Father Mallonee. "That's what the scriptures meant. The man could have changed into a werewolf."

David took Sadie by the hand and sat her down beside him on the couch. "So, do you believe it will happen again?" David asked the priest.

"We will soon find out, David."

Never Die On A Cold Night II
<u>REVELATIONS</u>

"Now I have a theory," David said, looking back and forth between Father Mallonee and Sadie. "You told me the man in black gave him a set of instructions to follow. You said the soldier was told to do these murders in a pattern isn't that right?"

"Yes, that's right. According to the instructions, the victim's locations must take the shape of a pentagram. If this murderer whether he or she is a werewolf or not, is doing the murders according to the design of a pentagram, we should know where the next murder is going to take place."

David looked at the priest with questioning eyes.

"What's the matter, David?" Sadie asked.

"The name. What was the soldier's name?"

"For the sake of his privacy, the name was withheld from the papers. However, I believe I can find out. Let me make a phone call," Father Mallonee said, getting up to look for a phone.

"It's in the bedroom," David told him.

About ten miles away from the hotel inside of the mobile headquarters the D.A.D. and two of his best men were listening in via satellite, to the conversation David and the priest had been having. And though there was not a smile on the D.A.D.'s face the men with him knew he was very pleased with what he was hearing.

"You two have done an excellent job setting up the surveillance. It has let us know something very important—how to find the wolf. Get me the map of Chicago let's see where this monster is going to strike next."

The man went to get the map of the Chicago while the radio man continued to tap into the conversations coming from David's hotel room.

"The man I am trying to get in touch with is not there, David, the priest said. "I was told he is on holiday with his family."

"I didn't know priest got married, Father," Sadie said.

"Most of them don't, but occasionally you will find one who will. In this man's case, it doesn't apply. He is not married. At any rate, we will have to wait until he gets home. I left a message for him to call me, so soon as I get the information, I'll get it to you. But I strongly feel you should stay at the monastery. You should be completely safe there until this is over."

"Maybe you're right, it might be best, David said. We should probably go now. There is no reason for me to stay here. While we are out, we can find a map maybe at a gas station and try to figure out where the next murder is going to take place."

David and his group left the hotel a few minutes later.

"Sir do you want us to do anything about David yet?" the young radio man asked.

"No, not yet. But make sure the three are kept under surveillance. I want to be apprised of every move David and his group make. If they separate, follow each one. This should prove very interesting."

"How do we handle the police tail on Sadie?" the radio man asked.

"Are they following her?" the D.A.D. asked.

Never Die On A Cold Night II
<u>REVELATIONS</u>

"No sir they lost her. They are searching for her now."

"That should let you know how much of a threat the police are to us," the D.A.D. confidently retorted.

"Well, what about Judith O'Brian? She tapped our radio transmission sir."

"Only by mistake. The FBI is no better than the police. Here they have the man they have been looking for all these years right under their noses, and my lord has hidden me from them. Never underestimate his abilities as the followers of the one with the nail prints in his hand have always done."

"No, sir, I promise I won't," the young man replied.

The D.A.D. plotted all of the murders that had occurred and begin to draw the pentagram the priest had spoken of with David about earlier.

In another part of town on the southeast side, David and his group had finally gotten to the monastery. Inside the building, they immediately started to put their heads together regarding the beast.

"You know, Father I don't completely believe this theory yet, but I know someone is killing these people. It may be we have a lunatic on our hands."

"Actually, I am not completely sure I believe it either. The church has come up with many things I have come to know are not the truth and because of that, I'm stuck here. So, it won't be the first time I've had to prove them wrong in my stubborn zeal to find the truth. It could be one of those times however strangely I don't think so. Now let's look at the map," Father Mallonee said as he put his reading glasses on.

When they moved most of their material over to the desk in the corner of his study Sadie spotted a computer on his desk. "Do you have a modem connected to your computer?" she asked.

"Yes, there is one, why do you ask?"

"I think we can do this a lot quicker if you let me use your computer."

"I'd let her do it, father. She's a Wonder-Woman on one of these things."

The priest pointed in the direction of the computer "By all means, help yourself. While she's on that, David, I want to show you something. I don't regret having never showed you this, but you may feel I should've."

The priest and David walked into his small living room, and he told David to sit down on the couch. He went into a closet and brought out a metal box. He walked over to David carrying the box in his hand and set it down on the coffee table in front of him. Then, sitting down in one of the chairs he let out a sigh of relief.

"What is this?" David asked not wanting to know the answer.

"It is your past, David," he said, smiling.

"Why didn't you show me this before?"

"Your mother asked me not to. But I think you should open it."

David reluctantly opened the metal box and looked inside. There was a small box inside with a large golden N on the top of it. He picked it up and opened it to reveal three gold rings on a velvet liner inside the box. Looking up at the priest tears started to form in his eyes. "These...were these my parent's rings?"

The priest nodded.

David held them in his hand for a while and placed them back gently inside the metal box. As he did this, he noticed the velvet platform supporting the rings moved a bit to where he could remove it. When he removed the platform with the rings, he saw an envelope underneath. After placing the velvet platform on the couch next to him, he reached into the box and pulled out the envelope. Apparently, it was never opened. The envelope revealed his name written on it in what he believed could have been his mother's handwriting. After opening the envelope, he pulled a letter out of it and began to read.

My Dearest Son David

   By the time you read this letter, you will be a grown man now and I will have been dead a long time. I truly am sorry I was not able to be there during most of your childhood, but it was beyond my control. However, I have the utmost confidence in Father Mallonee. I know he will—or shall I say he has done a—great job in raising you. At this point, I am writing you this letter because I am dying. I have instructed Father Mallonee not to tell you the reason of my death until after a certain time. So please don't ask him he knows when to tell you. David, I know you have an understanding heart, and you are a kind person, and I know you will do what is right. Forgive your father for leaving us. If he is still alive, make up with him and love him because he is your father. I know you will do this for me, darling, please understand that it is my dearest wish. Please remember me.

By
J. P. Leonard

Love always

Your Mother

David sat there staring at the letter for a while then placed it back in its envelope. His hands started to shake as he put the letter back into the envelope.

"What's the matter, David?" the priest asked. He watched David very closely. "Are you feeling okay?"

The shaking stopped, and David put the envelope holding his mother's letter down beside the box. "I'm fine, sir," he answered. He continued to carefully examine the contents of the box until he found a small package wrapped in a piece of notepaper with a ribbon around it. Opening the package, he discovered a set of pictures inside it. Pictures of a man and woman looking very happy together and some of them were with a small child. David reached over and handed the pictures to Father Mallonee." Are these my parents?"

"Yes, David. It's your father and mother. Those were the happier times."

"What happened to my father?" David asked remembering what his mother had written in the letter.

"At first I thought he was dead. We all thought he was dead up until I got word, he might still be alive. He was supposed to have died in the military in the Vietnam War, even though I heard he might be alive…well I don't know."

"Wait a minute now father you never told me my real father was in the military. Was he in the service at the time I was?"

Never Die On A Cold Night II
REVELATIONS

"David, your father, gave me instructions not to tell you he was in Vietnam. Then I lost contact with you before I heard he was dead I didn't hear from you again until recently."

Sadie walked into the room. "I think I've found where the next murder might be."

"We'll have to finish this discussion later David if you still want to."

"Yes, I do father. I want you to know I don't blame you for not telling me as it was my family's wishes that I stay in the dark. You were trying to continue to be a friend, and I understand."

Father Mallonee handed the pictures back to David. Sadie saw them and asked who they were.

"These are pictures of my parents," David said as he handed them to her.

Sadie's expression was one of disbelief. "Is this your father? Oh boy, David. If this is your father, then I know who he is. He's older now, but this is definitely him."

Father Mallonee and David looked at each other.

"Where did you see him?" David asked.

"I saw him at the police station once, but I met him at a banquet while you were gone. Since then, he and my mother have become a hot item. He goes by the name of Deputy Assistant Director Fitzgerald. He is working for the FBI."

"Ha! My father is working for the FBI?"

"That is hard to believe," the priest said. "I'm not saying I don't believe you, Sadie, it's just hard to believe he would be alive and not get in touch with me concerning David. Besides I was almost sure, he wasn't alive."

"He may already know where I am, Father. But I wonder why he hasn't gotten in touch with me. No matter we have more important things to do right now. Sadie, the computer—let's see what you found.

CHAPTER THIRTEEN

"How long will you live for me?"

Diana and Darren's police cruiser was making its second round.

"So, you don't think much of women who work, Officer Wilson?"

"Look I think you are intentionally turning my words around to put me on the defensive. Hey, pull over."

"Pull over for what?"

"I've got to take a leak," he said, a look of distress on his face.

"Can't you wait till we get to the station Officer Wilson?"

"No, I can't, Officer Belcher. Now if you please don't mind, I would like to take a leak right over there," he said pointing over to an abandoned building.

By
J. P. Leonard

"You know this is close to where your brother was..."

"I know. I've got something for him if he tries to get me."

"What is that?" Officer Belcher asked.

"I'll pee on him."

"Very funny, Darren. Do you want me to park by the building?"

"No park up here I'll be right back," he said as she pulled the car to the curb and turned her floodlights on the area. Darren got out of the car and shut the door and came around to the window on the driver's side. "You know I think you are kind of cute when you act so motherly but if you don't mind would you turn out the light?"

"I was just trying to be helpful," Diana said, pouting.

"Fine, but I don't need any help I've been doing this for quite a while now," he said as he headed down to the building. "I hate it when women think they always know what's right."

Darren hurriedly walked around the large building to the back of it out of the view of his partner. He stood by a dumpster and pulled his zipper down then began to relieve himself. The entrance to the back of the warehouse was about ten feet from where Darren was standing, and he had his back to it.

Shaking himself, he pulled up his zipper. At that moment he sensed it. Something was behind him. At first, he thought it was his playful yet concerned partner until he heard a low rumbling growl directly behind him sending a chill through him. Remembering his brother and all the other victims he knew it had to be an inhuman thing to kill this way.

Never Die On A Cold Night II
REVELATIONS

Darren's now trembling hand was slowly reaching for his .38 at his hip. How long had it been standing there? How long had he been standing there? If only he had listened to his partner. God, he thought, if you only let me out of this one, I will do right. I'll go to church or whatever you want me to do. He turned around to face his enemy but found nothing there. If something had been there, it was gone now. He was facing the open warehouse door and had a strong desire to investigate what might be inside. This time caution took over and stopped him from approaching the open warehouse door.

He figured he had better get back to the police car and call in some back up, because deep in his gut he knew something there. Turning around to go back the way he came he noticed a strong odor that he had not smelled before. He wondered if the sewer system had backed up somehow, but he continued to walk slowly back through the crates which had hidden him from view. Then he heard it again a low, rumbling growl, this time emitting from directly overhead. Pulling his gun out and aiming in the direction of the growl he immediately opened fire but whatever it was jumped over his head and down behind him before he could move. Although his instinct and quick reflexes caused him to turn and continue to fire it was too late. A huge, ugly, paw-like hand knocked the gun out of his hand with so much force he heard his wrist break at the joint. The pain was excruciating, but the fact that the beast had picked him up and was looking him straight in the eye made him temporarily forget the pain. Darren, making one last attempt tried to get free of the beast's grip by kicking it. Invariably only to make it mad. With the force of a hurricane, the beast threw him against the metal dumpster, and he heard his back snap in two like a pencil. He couldn't feel anything except for the blood coming up into his throat and gagging him. He prayed for a quick death.

The beast was immediately upon him. He could see the violent rage in the animal's eyes, and with all the strength he could muster he spit at it. Two seconds later his head was ripped from his body. The body twitched for a while then lay still on the cold ground. The beast, seeing what it had done cried out in a roar. Angry at the fact it had not kept to the instructions the werewolf began to tear the body to pieces. With fangs and razor-sharp claws, it tore into flesh and bones until the area and the ground around it was full of fresh blood and fragments of human tissue. Only the head lay whole at the entrance of the warehouse unnoticed by the beast.

Three blocks from the scene David and his group were searching for the location of the next murder. David had taken a small flashlight out of the glove compartment to look over the printout Sadie had gotten of the area locations found by the computer.

A police car sped past them with screaming sirens and flashing lights, and they knew something had happened.

"Follow the car, Sadie," David urged her.

"What if they see you?"

"They are not going to."

Sadie started to follow the police car. Another one came with screeching brakes from the side street emptying into their path it almost hit them. Sadie had to swerve to the side and up on the sidewalk to keep from being hit. She stopped the car suddenly, and David opened his door. He jumped out so quickly it startled her. He raced to Sadie's side of the door and motioned for her to get over.

"Get over Sadie I'll drive," David said, opening the car door at the same time.

Sadie moved over quickly, and David got in. With screeching tires, he backed the car off of the curb and pursued the police vehicle.

"What street is this?" David asked looking for a street sign.

"I don't know David I don't see a street sign," Sadie replied.

"We are definitely southeast. I think we better get out of here," Father Mallonee suggested.

"Yeah, you're right Father. But we've got to go to my place I've got to pick up something from there."

"David, are you sure? Couldn't I go for you or something? You could tell me where it is."

"I won't be able to explain it to you, I'll be alright. They won't think to find me there."

"The D.A.D. just told us to observe them and not try to apprehend," the radioman told the leader of the three hidden in the van. "He just wants us to follow him."

"So those are his orders," the leader said as he took the pair of binoculars down from his eyes. "It must be something about this priest." He had said it so low no one else had heard him.

"What did you say, sir?"

"Never mind just keep your distance but keep following him."

The radioman tapped the driver on his shoulder, and they drove off after David and his group.

The priest saw David repeatedly looking in his rear-view mirror. "What's the matter."

"Why hasn't Hanniz made his move yet I wonder?" David asked looking in the rearview mirror again. "Why hasn't he called the police like last time? I'm sure he called the police over to Sadie's and had me picked up. Why hasn't he done it yet? What is he waiting for?"

"What makes you think that's what's going to happen David?" Sadie asked.

"Because he wanted to frame David into joining him," the priest replied.

"So that's why they have been capturing and recapturing David. How could they keep on abducting you this way, David? More importantly, how can a group like this survive? With all the technology the police have and the FBI as well how is a group like the Red Pack able to exist?"

David spoke up to let them know. "They've got inside help. Judith O'Brian believed the Red Pack was responsible for certain assassinations during the sixties and are now the backers for certain other terrorist groups. Certain government officials would have to be responsible for the existence of the Red Pack."

"Yes, it's the only obvious conclusion I could come to and like you I don't understand why they haven't done anything," Father Mallonee said.

"We've got company," David said.

"Finally," Father Mallonee said.

"They've been behind us since we left my place," David replied. Sadie started to look around, but David grabbed her. "Don't look around, Sadie. We have got to act like we don't know they're there."

Sadie turned back around, and they drove on like no one knew a thing.

Inside the field office of D.A.D. Fitzgerald, the D.A.D. and everyone else was in a state of readiness. Another killing had taken place, and they had no murderer.

"You going to tell me you had authorization not to tell me why we hit the village?"

"Yes, sir, Deputy Assistant Director."

"The phone is not bugged, General, so there is no reason to call me that."

"Yes, sir. Sir we were authorized by your father not to tell you. I didn't know until a few days before your father's death the real reason for the incident. But I was bound by an allegiance to your father and would not have told you anyway. Your father was very specific. Your father didn't want you to be implicated in case any of this leaked to the public. You are much too important to have your position compromised."

"My father is—or shall I say my stepfather—is dead. Don't ever keep anything from me again or you will die. Is that clear, General?"

By
J. P. Leonard

"Yes, Sir I promise all my allegiance is to you, and it won't happen again."

"Now what was the German's last name?"

"We are working on it now, sir. The only records of the man to ever exist are with one of the priests who brought him from Cambodia, and the priest is somewhere on vacation, but we will find him. Our people are looking for him now.

David and his crew had gone back to Father Mallonee's home, and David was unwrapping the package he had taken from his apartment. It was the disks Sadie had made for him which had the three years' worth of murders. David put the disk into the computer but could not get them to show up on the screen.

"Sadie would you come here please," David said.

"The van following us is outside," Sadie told David as she walked over to him. "What are we going to do about it?"

"Nothing right now. I need you to help me bring this information up," David said, showing her what was on the screen.

"Here let me do it." She pushed David from his seat. "I'll call you when it's ready."

David walked over to the kitchen where Father Mallonee was and watched him while he began to prepare to cook fish in a skillet on the stove.

"I figured we might as well eat," he said as he slit the fish, he was holding down the middle of its belly and cleaned out the insides. "I have figured out the location of the next two murders or where the beast will strike next."

"How?" David asked as he sat down on one of the chairs at the table. "And now do you believe it's really—a wolfman?"

"Look at the map," the priest said pointing to the table. David gazed at the drawing of the circle, and the lines on the paper. It was the complete shape of a pentagram. "Depending on what we find out about tonight whether it was a murder and if the murder was the same, we can predict where the next two will occur."

"Are these the locations where you have the red X's marked?"

"Yes."

"You've marked this street. One of the locations is the very street we are on."

"That's right David and the fact time has almost run out lets me know it must be tomorrow night."

"That's right, the winter months are almost over. March twentieth is tomorrow, and the twenty-first is the beginning of spring."

The phone rang.

"Can you watch these fish, David? I'll be right back?"

Father Mallonee went into his study and left David in the kitchen.

David was taking the last piece of fish out of the skillet when he felt someone behind him. "Sadie you should have been doing this," he said thinking Sadie was behind him, and he wanted to tease her, but when he turned around, he almost jumped out of his skin. The woman he had seen all along was behind him.

By
J. P. Leonard

"Please help him if you don't, he'll die," the wearied woman pleaded.

"Help who, lady and how did you get in here?" David knew there was no way out of the kitchen except through the doorway, so he went to the doorway and called Sadie. But when he came back, the woman was gone.

"What's the matter, David?" Sadie asked when she came into the room.

"I saw her again, Sadie."

"You saw who David?"

"The woman—the one screaming out of the window. You saw her here?"

When David saw the doubt on her face, he calmly went over to her and took her by the hand guiding her to one of the chairs. They both sat down in the chairs and David looked into her eyes and calmly spoke to her. "Sadie it has finally occurred to me I might have some psychic ability. Every-time I see the woman a murder has occurred. Every-time, Sadie. Now, Father Mallonee believes there will be two more murders between now and tomorrow night. I have seen the woman again which proves it."

"Don't you think this could be stress or something, you've been through so much?"

David momentarily shook his head feeling alone. "It's what Father Mallonee thought the first time I came to him. But now he believes what is killing people could be a werewolf! I have also seen this thing in a vision or dream or something, and it seems I am someone else the beast is about to devour. Before it happens, I come out of it." David looked into her worried eyes and could feel how she felt. I don't want you to be afraid we will get this thing."

"How? You are not with the police now you are alone by yourself."

"That's not so." David gently took her hand in his. "I have you—and Father Mallonee. I am not alone." Convincing Sadie convinced himself that he was not alone.

Sadie smiled and leaned over to him and allowed his lips to brush against hers. He drew her to him, as his hand guided its way up her arm to her shoulder while the kiss became more intense. Suddenly they both heard a tremendous crash and Father Mallonee screamed David's name. Before she could say anything to David, he was up and running out of the kitchen but in the opposite direction of the scream. Sadie followed him into the living room and saw him go into his coat pocket and bring out a black .45.

"Stay here Sadie," David said pushing her back behind him. Just then another crash, and David ran in the direction of the scream. When he got there, he couldn't believe his eyes. There it was standing there in the middle of a destroyed study. Father Mallonee was against the wall, and the wolf was between David and him. It was huge, and it smelled foul. Although Father Mallonee's office ceiling was about ten feet tall, the monster had to crouch a little to stand.

David aimed his gun to shoot, but Father Mallonee raised his hand.

"No David, wait, don't shoot."

"I don't know, Father this thing has killed a lot of people."

"I know you don't want to hurt me," Father Mallonee said to the beast. "I know who you are, and I know I can help you.

By
J. P. Leonard

Your father was a good man, and I know you are a good person—inside. You are a good person inside, but the devil has tricked you. I can help you."

David stepped a little closer.

"Stop, David." But it was too late. It turned with the quickness of a gazelle before David could get a shot off. The beast jumped through the window that it had come in and ran off into the darkness.

"You should have let me kill it, Father."

"In the house of God; no such thing, my son! No, we must try to help it," Father Mallonee said as he picked up a chair from the floor and sat it upright. "Where did you get the gun anyway?"

"Out of Janet's apartment," David remembered Sadie and started to go back to her. Just as he put the gun down on the table, there was a crash behind him, and something hit him in his back and knocked him out of the room. He heard a short gasp for air, a scream and a thump, and the head of Father Mallonee rolled to the doorway of the hall. David could smell the foul stench come from the beast. It was all he could do to get up off the floor. Sadie came rushing towards him and helped him to his feet.

"You have got to get out of here!" David shouted. "I don't want you to get hurt."

"I'm not going without you," Sadie said. Then they both heard a blood-curdling howl. "God David, what is it?"

David didn't answer he just grabbed her and ran through the hall into the living room and out into the next hall. They were running as fast as they could. "We got to make it to the car," he said.

Never Die On A Cold Night II
REVELATIONS

"Wait," she said, trying to pull him to a stop. "I don't have my keys! They're in my coat inside the closet!"

David swore for the first time in front of Sadie. "I've got to go back in there and get it."

David and Sadie were standing in the middle of the sanctuary and David tried to get her to wait there.

"What happened to Father Mallonee David?"

"I thought you saw it."

"Saw what?"

David hesitated for a minute. "He's dead. He's dead Sadie. It was horrible. The most hideous thing I have ever seen. I didn't believe something so hideous could exist in the real world. It's not like the movies; it's not like that. I could hardly bear to look at it. I've got to go back in to get the keys. So, you've got to be brave and go back in with me. Because I don't want to leave you out here."

"Do you think it's still in there?"

"I don't know."

"David I can feel your hands trembling. I've never seen you like this before. Now I'm afraid."

"Good. This way we might get out of this alive."

They started on their way back inside the apartment of their now deceased friend. Fearing what they would see inside did not keep them from going back. David knew the beast would chase them and bring them down on foot. The beast had not come through the apartment after them, and it made David believe it was gone.

After finding the keys and getting their coats, David told Sadie
to wait in the upper part of the hall near the study. He didn't want
Sadie to see Father Mallonee. As he entered the study, he could
see blood and pieces of flesh everywhere. His best friend and the
only father he had ever known was gone. How could God let a
beast like this exist in a world as fragile as it was? Then he
remembered the feel of darkness all around him everywhere he
went. It seemed as if everything was out of whack, as if he and
Sadie were the only sane people left. Looking at the floor, he
saw the .45 still there on the table and picked it up and put it in
the back of his pants, and walked out of the room, closing the
door behind him. Getting Sadie, they went back out into the
sanctuary and out the front door. As soon as they stepped on to
the front walk, lights came on from everywhere and hit them in
the face.

"Hold your fire it's David," a deep, heavy voice said from
inside the circle of men surrounding the parish. David quickly
put Sadie behind him and pulled out his .45 pointing it in the
direction of the voice.

"What's the matter, David?"

"Hanniz is out there."

"Hanniz? Who is Hanniz?" Sadie asked.

Then he heard a familiar voice call out to him from the lights.
"David it's me, Judith. Please drop your weapon no one is going
to hurt you. I give you my word."

"We give you our word," the male voice said again. Only it
wasn't as deep as before.

"David it's the D.A.D. It's your father, David. It's your

father."

David remembered what the letter said. What his mother had wanted him to do. Why had his mother asked this of him? He didn't want to do it but love for his mother made him want to try as much as he could. David put his gun back behind him he grabbed Sadie and started towards the voice he had heard. Fitzgerald motioned for his men to go into the parish as David stepped behind the lights.

"It's gone," David said as he stared the D.A.D. in the eye. He was a cold looking man and it didn't seem as if he cared if David were there or not. Not one hint he loved him or hated him or thought anything about him David thought.

"David, I have to place you under arrest for crimes against the government. Take his weapon and pat him down." The D.A.D. told one of the men.

David allowed himself to be patted down while another man started to put handcuffs on him. Judith was watching from a distance.

"That won't be necessary," he told his man. "He's not going anywhere."

"I know who you are...father."

"Such a polite title," Fitzgerald seeming to joke but it was rather unnatural because he didn't smile.

"Then what am I supposed to call you?"

"I don't care. What do you want to call me?"

"Some choice words come to mind."

"David," Sadie said.

David shook his head and chuckled out loud. "Why do you want me now. After all this time?" He walked closer to the D.A.D. One of the men started to step in between them, and the D.A.D. slapped the man so hard he fell to the ground.

"Don't ever come between my son and me again," he shouted to the man.

David stepped closer to his father and stood right in his face. He spoke to him in a low voice where so only he and Fitzgerald could hear. "You sound like the man who captured me. Are you?"

"I am the man who saved you. The police wanted you in jail, and they still do. I protected you from them."

"You killed my friends," David snapped.

"I am your only family," the D.A.D. replied.

David walked away from the man, furious at what his mother wanted him to do. How could she not know what he was? And if she did, how could she ask such a thing? Judith walked over to David, but Sadie walked in front of her and grabbed his arm.

"The man is a monster, Sadie."

"He's still your father. No matter what he's done you can't change your roots."

"He's responsible for so many deaths, there is no telling what all his group is responsible for. And look, he's in the government. Our government. There is no wonder it's so corrupt. With men like him running our lives. The American dream will never be the same."

Never Die On A Cold Night II
REVELATIONS

"What do you think our presidents have done? What about World War II? All those Japanese killed. Innocent women and children all dead because we wanted to win a war," she said.

"But that was necessary. Hitler was trying to take over the world, and Japan bombed us first Sadie."

"Tell it to the dead children. Besides you don't know if he is Hanniz."

David tried to pull his arm away not because he was right but because it wasn't what he wanted to hear. But Sadie held on.

"All I'm saying is there are people all over making decisions for the majority and hurting the minority in the process. But if it weren't for the government, the world would be in chaos."

Fitzgerald walked over to where Sadie and David were standing. "All right enough of this philosophizing, we have a situation in the real world. The way I see it, David, we have a wolf on our hands that is going to strike somewhere between now and tomorrow morning. It's the last chance this year it's going to have to become completely human. And we need to find its whereabouts. So far, it's killed eleven people, right?"

"Yes, you're right. It has killed eleven people."

By then, Captain Edwards had gotten to the scene. When he spotted David, a big smile came across his face. "So, we finally caught you. Good work Fitzgerald," he said trying to appear grateful. "I'll take it from here. Sergeant take this man into custody."

"Hold on, Edwards," D.A.D. Fitzgerald said in a low and very calm voice. "I already have custody of this man."

"On whose authority," the captain angrily shouted. "He's not even in handcuffs. What if he runs off like he did the last time?"

"It's the federal government's call. David is our witness."

"Witness to what?" the Captain fumed.

"A witness to the murder of Father Mallonee by the werewolf," the D.A.D. added.

"The werewolf? You have got to be kidding?"

"I don't kid, Edwards."

"Fitzgerald do you think I'm stupid."

"No, I don't, but sometimes you outdo yourself. We have all this on tape. You want to hear it."

The captain looked at the D.A.D. for a while. Everyone could see the contempt and anger he had in his eyes toward Fitzgerald. "Fine, you want to take charge, he's all yours, why don't you handle it all." The captain stormed away.

It had started to get light outside.

"I think we all had better get some sleep," the D.A.D. said.

"What about David?" Sadie asked the D.A.D.

"You can have him for now," Fitzgerald said with a twinkle in his eye. "But he's mine tonight." Turning to David, he looked him in the eye. "You know the beast may want you tonight."

"What makes you think so? The instructions did not say who it must kill," David reminded the D.A.D.

"No, it didn't," he said seriously. "But I have a feeling—just be careful."

Never Die On A Cold Night II
<u>REVELATIONS</u>

"How can I? You have my gun?"

The D.A.D. motioned to one of his men. "Give him his weapon."

The man gave David the gun and David stood for a minute then put his arm around Sadie. "Wait for me in the car." Sadie left, and then David walked over to his father with his weapon down by his side. "Mom left me a note and said to love you, and I am going to try to do as she requested," he said as he put his weapon behind his back into his pants. "But I just want you to know it's under heavy protest by my conscience."

"A letter huh?" Fitzgerald's said as his cold eyes stared into David's. "What if I told you I wrote the letter?"

"What? You wrote the letter. You know you're something. Here I am about to give you my heart, and you knock it down and step on it."

"I don't want your heart; I want your allegiance."

Fitzgerald walked over to one of his men took the man's radio from him and handed it to David.

"What's this for?"

"You may need to call me."

David took the radio nodded and started to walk away from him. He stopped and turned to look at his father. "You are too much, old man." Then he turned back and continued to walk to Sadie."

From a distance, he saw Judith standing by the car talking with Sadie. Just before he got there, they had looked at him and started laughing.

"What's so funny?" David asked the two of them.

"Don't mind us, darling, it's just woman talk," Sadie said, smiling at Judith.

"Oh, I see," David said. He felt a little uneasy with them both standing there. "Well, I guess we'd better go now."

"Wait, David, Judith and I were talking, and she came up with something that might interest you. But I'll let her tell you."

Judith cocked her head to the side and put on a sexy smile. It made David wonder about their conversation together. "I think we should all sleep together."

"What? You're kidding me. Are you crazy?" David said.

"Not in the same bed, David," Sadie said. "She wants us to stay in her command module with her."

Judith nodded. "We have the equipment to be able to track this thing when it comes into the vicinity of the mobile headquarters which can be placed in the area where the beast must come. We can be ready for it."

It all made sense to David. He would be right there when the beast attacked. "All right, Judith you have got us for the night," David agreed.

"I want you to know David I told Sadie about my interest in you, but you had made your choice to be with her, and I respect your decision. If you are happy with Sadie, then I am happy for you. I mean it I really am. So, I'm hoping we can all be friends."

"I see no problem with being friends do you?" Sadie asked David then watching for his reaction.

"No, not at all. Now, are we finished here? Ladies, I'm bushed."

"I will ride with you over to the trailer and you two can get a few hours' sleep," Judith said

At first, none of them were able to sleep. Instead, they went back to Judith's trailer and set things up. The trailer was positioned in the vicinity where the beast might strike next, by using the coordinates Sadie had. Fitzgerald's trailer was positioned about a mile away from Judith's trailer while the police made a complete circle around the area. They worked for hours setting up sophisticated sensors to detect the movement of anyone coming into the area. Security was very tight—they all meant to catch themselves a wolfman. Finally, around four o'clock in the afternoon went to bed to get some much-needed rest.

By
J. P. Leonard

CHAPTER FOURTEEN

"The conclusion of the whole matter?"

About nine o'clock that night David was awakened by a soft kiss on his lips. He opened his eyes to find Sadie sitting on the edge of the couch he was laying on. At first, he thought he had been dreaming until he surveyed his surroundings and realized he was in Judith's trailer.

"How was it sleeping with Judith?" A tired David Neal asked Sadie as he stretched himself and let out a big yawn.

Sadie laid her head on his uncovered hairy chest. "Not as fun as it would have been with you."

Chuckling David put his hand up behind his head. "Yeah you're right Sadie," he said putting his arms down around her. "I can't wait until this is all over. By the way, is our hostess still sleep?"

"No," Sadie replied. "She left, saying something about—

shopping or something."

"Women," David said shaking his head. "Even in a crisis, they can still find time to shop."

Sadie sat up quickly and smacked him hard on the chest. "What do you mean?"

"Ouch, you can hit pretty hard."

There was a knock on the door. David went to the door and opened. It was the radioman.

"Someone just called and said the D.A.D. had a heart attack. They told us to notify you."

"David, your father."

"Who was it who called?" David asked.

"Someone from his trailer," the radioman said as he left to go back to his post.

David walked away from the door. Sadie shut the door and watched him go back to the couch. "What are you going to do?" she asked.

"What do you want me to do Sadie?"

"It's your father. He could be dying."

"Sadie, I think he's the man everybody have been hunting. I believe he's Hanniz."

"How do you know? Do you have any proof? Did he tell you he was?"

"He just as much told me he was."

"But he also told you he wrote the letter. And you know he didn't."

"No. Mother wrote the letter."

"Then I think he's just playing some game with you because he doesn't know how to show affection and maybe all this is hard to deal with."

"You know, you're probably right."

"Yes, I'm right. Now you go see your father I'll be here when you get back."

He got himself together and left the trailer. Judith was pulling up in her car. Getting out of the car and taking some bags out it and when she saw David.

"What's the matter, David?"

"It's Fitzgerald he's had a heart attack."

"What? Are you sure?"

"Yeah, we just got the call."

"How are you going to go?" Judith asked with a concerned look on her face.

David looked around. "Where is Sadie's car?"

"We left it at the last place we had the trailer, remember."

David swore. It was the second time he'd done it.

"Look David take my car. I'll stay here with Sadie."

She walked over and gave him the keys.

Never Die On A Cold Night II
REVELATIONS

"Thanks, Judith you're really a good sport about all this."

"Sure. Friends remember? I'll see you when you get back."

David got into the car and drove away. About halfway to Fitzgerald's trailer, he saw a woman standing right in the path of his vehicle and put on the brakes swerving to a stop. As David got out of the car he noticed it was the old woman, he kept seeing. She looked up into the dark moonlit sky and then back at him again. "It's too late now," she said and disappeared.

David stood staring at the spot where he had seen the old woman wondering what she meant. Then, remembering the reason, he was there he got back in the car and decided to use the radio he had been given. Turning the radio on David spake into it. "This is David Neal calling for Fitzgerald."

"Yes, David," Fitzgerald responded.

"You sound o.k. to me," David said feeling confused. "Someone said you were having a heart attack.

"David listen to me. We know who the wolf is. Where are you?"

"I'm in a car on my way to you. Why…who is it?"

"When you and Sadie get here, I'll fill you in."

"Sadie's not with me, she's with Judith."

"Look, David, I want you to be calm—Sadie is in grave danger. We found out that the father found out the daughter had been staying with the two priests all that time. After the father found his daughter was safe there, he decided to stay but then after a while he left, thinking the daughter was cured. He knew he wasn't, and so he decided to go back to Cambodia to get away

By
J. P. Leonard

from her believing he might kill her. She was then sent to stay with foster parents. Get this, David—the foster parent's name was O'Brian. The daughter's name is Judith O'Brian. She's the werewolf, David. Judith O'Brian is the werewolf. David...David, you hear me?"

But David had thrown the radio down and with screeching tires he turned the car around and started back to the trailer. He remembered what the woman he saw in the vision had said. 'It's too late now.' "No! No!" he shouted. Then David screamed Sadie's name. He started to shake again just as he did in the priest's house. He also felt a sharp, hard pain in his chest.

Then, from out of nowhere, he heard a voice. "Bring him out of it now. Now, I said, he's having a heart attack. Bring him out now."

David had the trailer in sight, but what was the voice? Gripping his chest with his hand and driving with the other he had just about made it to the trailer. Just before he could get out the whole sky began to get brighter and brighter. "What is this?" he said aloud. The trailer, the street, and everything else—were being taken over by this great white light. Just as David closed his eyes because of the intensity of the light, he felt a jolt in his head then darkness.

Seconds later he opened his eyes, and the light started to flood his eyes. Then he saw them, men and women with white coats on running around him, wires and machines everywhere. Some wires were running from his body and some back to computerized machines. Just as he started to ask himself where he was, he started to remember. The men and women running around started to become familiar to him. Then there was Charley—no there was Doctor Williams. Doctor James Williams standing beside him smiling. "I know you," David said, smiling. "I remember now. It's all coming back to me. What happened?

Never Die On A Cold Night II
REVELATIONS

Why did you bring me out?" He started to pull all the wires from his body. He was laying on a white sterile table. He tried to stand up but felt a little dizzy and sat back down.

"Here, let me help you, David." Doctor Williams grabbed David's arm and helped him back to the table.

"How's my wife?" he said, holding his head in his hand then taking a deep breath.

"She's fine, David. It was touch and go for a minute. We thought we'd lost her, but she's fine now. She asked about you, too."

"That's my Sadie."

David thought about the experiment. "James that was the most exciting trip I have ever taken in my life. It was so real, the dream was so real."

"It almost killed you, too," Dr. Williams told him.

"A minor adjustment, James. A minor adjustment. All we need to do when she gets to the more intense parts back down power to the chip. You know, just like turning the volume down. It would have been all we needed to do, and we could have continued." David was back to himself again, and he felt good. "James we are going to be rich," he said putting his shirt on.

"Are you sure we can correct the problem in time for production, David? I'd hate to see on the evening news that people were dying from this thing."

"Don't worry," David said, smiling. "I know exactly what the problem is. We've got a winner here."

Doctor Chase entered the room. "Doctor Neal you made it just in time. We had just gotten the call while you were under. Unless you produced something, they would have had to shut us down. It was one of the first cuts they were going to make. But you did it. You did it. You ought to be proud of yourself."

"How long were we under, James?" David asked impatiently.

Dr. James looked at his watch. "About two hours and fifty-three minutes to be exact for the both of you."

David looked up at him. "Who else went under? I didn't authorize anybody else." David walked over to a mirror hanging on a wall near the door and looked in his eyes.

"Why don't you let us, sir?" James said following David around like a little puppy.

David looked at him. "You were a pretty crazy guy in there James." He walked over to the computer terminal and started to look at the program. "I asked you James who else went under. And where is Sadie?"

"With your daughter, sir."

David heard a banging outside the door. He jumped. "What is all the noise?"

"It's just Fitzgerald. You know the janitor. He's mopping the floor out there now. He must have knocked on the door."

"What's he doing out there now?"

"Sir you told him to do it."

"I wish you would stop calling me sir. You are making me nervous. Did someone turn the air-conditioning up? It's cold in here." David said as he picked up a notebook and started to write in it.

"Sir…uh, David you need to let us check you out."

"Did you check my wife out?"

"No, but—"

"Then you don't need to check me out either."

Doctor Chase had been talking to one of the technicians and had overheard the conversation between David and Dr. Williams. He walked over to David. "What is this competitive thing between you and Sadie? You act like children sometimes."

David just smiled and ignored him.

"You know it's evident why your daughter acts the way she does."

"Where is my daughter. She's usually in here bothering me by now. Where is Karen."

"Didn't Dr. Williams tell you?" Doctor Chase said smiling and looking at Dr. Williams.

Sadie came in. "Wasn't the journey tremendous darling?"

"Sadie!" David said very glad to hear her voice. He got up from the computer terminal and went over to her and grabbed her giving her a long, slow kiss. Letting her go he grabbed her hand and walked over to the mainframe with pride. "Sadie, we did it. You are looking at the first Biofeedback Environmental Thought Transferring Interface in the history of the free world. Now all anyone needs to do is put one of these thought transferrers on," he said, picking up the head device. "Turn it on and close their eyes and 'voila' an instant movie is created, with themselves as the main characters. And if they want their friends to join in, they all become characters in the movie, all believing their real lives are the lives the computer is producing."

"It's great, David," Sadie said smiling.

"James, were you able to keep track of the whole dream sequence?" Sadie asked.

"Yes, we were. Every part of the sequence you experienced the sounds the way the characters looked the scenery everything. We saw and recorded the whole thing."

"What about the part where Judith went back to kill me did you see it?"

"No, and neither did you."

"That's right," she said smiling. "That is right. I remember David coming back to the trailer but nothing else. I remember it just like I watched it on tv."

"Yes, essentially you will remember everything just like a movie created by actors only this one is by computer. There will have to be some adjustments made but all in all, it was a success."

Doctor Chase came over to the computer. "So, this will supply how many homes?"

David walked over to the railing and looked over the railing down to the bottom of the computer twenty feet down to approximately ten feet above their heads. "There is no number Dr. Chase. The number is infinite."

"So essentially you could have a million a billion dreams created all at once?"

Never Die On A Cold Night II
<u>REVELATIONS</u>

"Right," David answered. "Betti can do it. Betti with an I."

"Makes sense," Dr. Chase said.

David smiled proudly.

Then the phone rang once, then twice.

"Is somebody getting the phone?" David shouted.

One of the technicians answered it.

"She's marvelous!" Dr. Chase said proudly.

"It's intensive care, Dr. Neal. They said Karen is going to be fine."

"What? What is this about Karen? What was wrong with Karen?"

"Calm down, honey. I saw Karen already, and she's okay. I told her to lay down for twenty more minutes, she's supposed to come in afterward," Sadie said.

David looked around at everyone angrily. "If any of you ever keep something like this from me again, I'll fire you. I am going to go see my daughter. Who did she play?"

James looked at the clipboard he was carrying. "Diana...Diana Belcher, the policewoman."

David smiled. "Just like her old dad. Okay, I'll be back." David rushed to the door.

"Honey be careful the floor was just—" Before she could finish the sentence to warn him, he had run out to the hall, slipped on the slippery floor and fell face down on the floor. The last thing he heard before he blacked out was the sound of police sirens and many voices. But one sound stood out clearly. "It's too late he's gone."

Detective David Neal lay on the cold, icy slush-filled street of Chicago where he had tripped and fell. His body close to death but his brain still sending out faint electrical impulses.

"Do you think we could have gotten to him in time?" one of the ambulance drivers said to the other one.

"I don't see how. He's not breathing his heart has stopped. He's dead."

"Then how is it possible rigor mortis hasn't set in?" the ambulance driver asked.

"I don't know. Maybe because of the cold and his head laying on the ice. I don't know, I'm not a doctor."

"Who were those guys who shot his partner anyway?"

"Who knows? I heard these guys worked undercover a lot. Some of those guys on the street you don't mess with," the second paramedic said.

"Who's the lady over there?" the driver asked.

The second paramedic looked up. "I don't know some bag lady, I guess. Hey, look here comes their captain."

"Sergeant, did you take the woman's complete statement?" Captain Edwards asked.

"Yes, sir what a waste," the officer stated.

"Yes, I know, officer, but about the statement..."

"Yes sir, she said one of the men, David Neal got out of his car and went around the back. Slipped and fell on the ground and must have hit his head because he just lay there. Then three men in a black van drove up and got out of their van walked over to Charley grabbed him and beat him up then shot him and left him for dead."

"When did this happen?"

"We don't know captain, maybe hours ago?"

"Who called it in Sargent?" the captain asked.

"A lady just driving by coming from work called it in."

"Why didn't the woman who saw everything call it in, is she homeless or something?"

"No sir she lives across the street," he said pointing in the direction of the building standing there. "She just doesn't have a phone."

"My God, man. This is a normally very busy street, but because of this blizzard-like cold, these men lay here dead for hours. What a waste," the captain said. He looked at the woman. "You better get her to the precinct—ah what is she saying she keeps repeating something can you hear what she's saying."

"Yes, sir it sounds like she's saying, 'It's too late now.'

The captain looked away from the woman hearing a commotion going on between the first ambulance driver and the driver of a second ambulance which had just got there. Wondering what was going on he and the Sargent walked over to the drivers.

"You just made a mistake. Own up to it and let's get both men to the hospital right away," said one of the paramedics of the second ambulance. Both sets of paramedics worked feverishly to get David and Charley into the ambulances, David in one and Charley into the other.

The Sargent shouted out. "What are you men doing, aren't they both dead?"

"No, neither of them is dead," the driver of the second ambulance said. And with that, he got into his emergency vehicle and with sirens blaring both ambulances sped away to Chicago's General Hospital. By the time the captain and many of his men and women from the precinct had gotten there a distraught Janet Stilles, and her daughter Theresa were talking to one of the doctors. The two Stilles women were hugging each other very tightly, waiting until the doctor finished talking to them. Afterward, they both began to weep violently.

Captain Edwards caught up with the Doctor who had just been standing there and saw the defeated look on the doctor's face. "There was nothing we could do," the doctor said to captain Edwards. "We just got him too late." Standing there beside the doctor was the head nurse. As the doctor sadly walked away, the nurse stayed behind and moved closer to the captain.

"The other man is alive," she said to the captain.

"Detective David Neal is alive," he asked? The hurtful frown he had went away and a smile took its place. He respected both men, and he was very sad to hear that one of his most excellent detectives had passed. At the same time knowing David was alive was a weight off his heart.

"He's in emergency right now, but his wife is in the Chapel, that's all I know," the nurse said as she walked back to her station.

Captain Edwards tried to find Janet but learned she had left the hospital along with her Daughter. The officers who came with the captain walked up to him after finding out Charley was gone. They didn't know the prognosis of Detective Neal. "Charley is gone," the captain said to the officers.

"Yes, we know," one of the officers confirmed. "But what about David?" one of the other officers hurriedly asked.

"He's in surgery, no I mean he's still in emergency," the captain responded. "Anyone of you know where the chapel is?" Another nurse was walking by, and the captain asked her where the location of the chapel might be. He rushed to it. Captain Edwards walked into the chapel and saw a young woman in front, sitting on the bench with her head lowered. The woman appeared to be praying, so he stopped and waited while lowering his head. He thought about Charley, and then about his own wife who died a couple of years past, and he almost wept until he saw the woman raise her head.

At the same time, a young doctor walked past him and down the aisle where the woman was sitting and began to speak to her. Momentarily someone tapped the captain on his shoulder. The captained turned to see one of his other detectives standing there.

"Captain, I thought you would want to know."

"What is it, detective?"

"We got em. We got one of the guys who shot, Charley. After we got the description from the woman, we tracked down the van from the plate numbers she provided, and we are on our way to get the other two gangbangers who were with him."

"Alright detective, good job. I'll meet you at the station as soon as I can get there."

"Alright boss," he said, as he left the chapel.

By
J. P. Leonard

The woman quickly got up and started to get her things to follow the doctor until she saw the captain. Walking up to the captain she stood in front of him with a large smile on her face. "David, is awake and asking for you and me."

"I'm glad, Sadie, let's go see him."

When Sadie and Captain Edwards entered the hospital room, David's, doctor was still there. Sadie quickly ran over to David, grabbed him and kissed him gently on the lips.

"I'm glad to see you. I have something to tell you about what I experienced while I was laying on the ground there in the cold."

"What do you mean?" she asked, looking at him and then the doctor.

The doctor interrupted. "Sadie what David wants to tell you is while he was out, he had a mental episode."

Looking at the doctor very curiously, she asked. "What type of mental episode?"

"Well, he was in a dream state for…"

Captain Edwards interrupted. "Doctor I'm sorry, but I have to interrupt you, I need to tell David and Sadie…"

But David interrupted the captain at that point. "Captain I know—Charley is dead."

"But David how did you…"

"Charley is dead?" Sadie asked as she abruptly sat down on the edge of the bed and looked over at him. "And who told you David? Did the doctor?"

Never Die On A Cold Night II
REVELATIONS

"No Sadie," the doctor responded. "No one from the hospital told David, he told me."

"But how?" the captain asked. "I thought he was knocked out. Hell, I thought he was dead."

"He was dying sir," the doctor explained. And at that time Charley was not deceased but still alive."

"Look this is too strange for me," the captain said, looking over at David. "Son, I'm glad you are alive, and I hope you're ok, but I've got to go and…

David interrupted again. "I know captain—to put away some bad guys. You or shall I say the detectives on the case found the gang members who beat up and shot Charley."

There was silence in the room as all three of them stared at the man, detective David Neal lying there smiling at them.

Sixty days after the funeral for Charley Stilles, David having told Sadie about his revelations, what he had went through while laying on that cold ground, the dreams and visions made her distrustful and wonder, being confused about how it all could be possible. She watched David from their bed as he got himself ready for work. His doctor had told her after she had come to his office what might have happened to him, even though he couldn't explain the clairvoyant episodes.

"David suffered some temporary damage to the front part of his brain," he explained but went on to say. "This is called the frontal lobe. It controls memory, thinking, and learning. The front part of his skull where he fell received a small fracture; something that in time would heal. However, he did also receive a concussion, and it was a bit severe. This disabled him for a time. After he was awakened, he told me of the long dream he had which seemed to him to last for several months. In reality, it only lasted for some hours."

The doctor went on to say," I once read in a journal a young man who had a dream where he lived for two years, but when he had awaken, he'd only been sleeping for only a number of hours. He claimed he had a family in the dream, he had never seen before, but in the dream, he knew them—all of them. What that man claimed to have gone through sounds a lot like what your husband Detective Neal experienced. Just as this man said it was very real to him, your husband claimed the same thing. Now I am not saying your husband lied, all I am saying it's not the norm for people to have had dreams where they have spent a long period of time in them. Now as far as the front part of the brain is concerned, it also receives and interprets from the five senses. The trauma to it may have caused what we witnessed in his room. Frankly, if I had not witnessed it with my own eyes and heard it with my own ears, I would never have believed it."

Sadie would never have either, but there she was now sitting on the bed watching someone who happened to be her husband whom she witnessed having a clairvoyant episode.

"Honey," David said, wanting to get her attention as he finished dressing. "Where are you, what's going on in that mind of yours?"

"Oh, I'm here David. I was just thinking."

David walked over to the bed and sat down in front of her. After David's clairvoyant episodes, which lasted only a week, he had not had another. Sadie was glad all of that was over. She

Never Die On A Cold Night II
REVELATIONS

wanted her husband back. After his accident, she was worried about what the doctor told her, and she just wanted things to be normal. Like the time they made love in the park after they had gotten married. Now everything was like a freak show with them, and it was if she was waiting for the proverbial shoe to drop. The people they both worked with had been playfully ribbing them. They had started asking him to find things for them or asking stuff like what the next lottery numbers were going to be. Some of the women she worked with, asked her to ask David when they were going to get pregnant and what the child's sex is going to be and frankly, she was tired of it all. After while her boss made them stop doing it and she was glad. She just wanted things back to normal—she just wanted her old David back.

"Are you sure you're ok Sadie?" he asked.

"Yes, David," she said with an assuring smile.

David started smiling back.

"What are you smiling about David?"

"How would you like to go on vacation say for about two weeks? I do have the time coming to me, and so do you. Besides, we have been married for a couple of months and haven't gone on our honeymoon yet."

"Ok, honey," Sadie responded. "Let's start putting something together after we talk to our bosses. I'm ready if you are."

"Ok," he said giving her a sweet peck on the lips as he got up and hurriedly made his way out to the stairs. "I've got to go to work."

"Ok...but don't forget to get something to eat from the kitchen." She got up to look for the pink pumps, she wanted to wear that day. She thought she had put them in her bedroom closet, but when she looked, she didn't see them.

As David was getting ready to go out to the garage, he shouted to Sadie. "They are in the living room closet where you left them."

"Ok, thanks, babe—wait a minute," she shouted. "I didn't tell you I was looking for them." She started stomping her feet and shouting his name. "D A V I D, D A V I D." But it was too late he was already gone. And so was Sadie—just right out of her mind.

*** THE END? ***